KU-685-932

"You're A Wicked Influence, Aaron,"

she said mischievously, for the first time sounding as if she had let down her guard with him.

"Wicked is more fun, and you know you agree," Aaron said softly, standing close in front of her. "I'll show you tonight when we're together."

"Oh, no, you won't. I don't need you to show me one thing. We'll have dinner, talk a little and say good night. That's the agenda. Got it?"

"Oh, I have an agenda. I had it the moment I walked through the door and saw you sitting there with Cole. My agenda is to get you to take down your hair."

"Amazing. One of my goals is to keep my hair pinned up, so one of us is going to fail completely," she said, her blue eyes twinkling.

Eager to be with her for the whole evening, to flirt and dance and hopefully kiss, he leaned a bit closer. "If I placed my fingers on your throat, I'll bet I'd feel your pulse racing. You want the same thing I do."

00 401 063 620

Long 8/22
2928-1/23
ES 19/23
9433-5/23
9458-9/23

Pregnant
by the Texan

SARA ORWIG

MILLS BOON®

All rights reserved including the right of reproduction
in whole or in part in any form. This edition is published
by arrangement with Harlequin Books S.A.

This is a work of fiction. Names, characters, places,
locations and incidents are purely fictional and bear no
relationship to any real life individuals, living or dead, or
to any actual places, business establishments, locations,
events or incidents. Any resemblance is entirely
coincidental.

This book is sold subject to the condition that it shall
not, by way of trade or otherwise, be lent, resold, hired
out or otherwise circulated without the prior consent
of the publisher in any form of binding or cover other
than that in which it is published and without a similar
condition including this condition being imposed on the
subsequent purchaser.

® and TM are trademarks owned and used by the
trademark owner and/or its licensee. Trademarks
marked with ® are registered with the United Kingdom
Patent Office and/or the Office for Harmonisation in the
Internal Market and in other countries.

First published in Great Britain 2014
by Mills & Boon, an imprint
Large Print edition 2015
Eton House, 18-24 Paradise Road,
Richmond, Surrey, TW9 1SR

Northamptonshire
Libraries

© 2014 Harlequin Books S.A.

Special thanks and acknowledgement are given
to Sara Orwig for her contribution to the
Texas Cattleman's Club: After the Storm miniseries.

ISBN: 978-0-263-25980-3

Harlequin (UK) Limited's policy is to use papers that
are natural, renewable and recyclable products and made
from wood grown in sustainable forests. The logging
and manufacturing processes conform to the legal
environmental regulations of the country of origin.

Printed and bound in Great Britain
by CPI Antony Rowe, Chippenham, Wiltshire

SARA ORWIG

lives in Oklahoma. She has a patient husband who will take her on research trips anywhere, from big cities to old forts. She is an avid collector of Western history books. With a master's degree in English, Sara has written historical romance, mainstream fiction and contemporary romance. Books are beloved treasures that take Sara to magical worlds, and she loves both reading and writing them.

With a big thank you to Stacy Boyd,
Harlequin Desire Senior Editor,
and Charles Griemsman,
Harlequin Desire Series Editorial.
Also, with love to my family.

One

Early in December as the private jet came in for a landing, Aaron Nichols looked below. Even though the tornado had hit two months earlier, the west side of Royal, Texas, still looked unrecognizable.

No matter how many times he had gone back and forth between Dallas and Royal, he was shocked by the destruction when he returned to Royal. The cleanup had commenced shortly after the storm, but the devastation had been too massive to get the land cleared yet. Hopefully, he and his partner, Cole Richardson, could find additional ways for R&N Builders to help in the restoration. As he looked at the debris—the broken lumber, bits and pieces of wood and metal, a crumpled car with the front half torn away—he thought of the lives wrecked and changed forever. It was a reminder of his own loss over seven years ago that had hit as suddenly as a storm: a car accident, and then Paula and seventeen-month-old Blake were gone. With time the pain had dulled, but it never went away and in moments like this when he had a sharp reminder, the hurt and memories hit him with a force that sometimes made him afraid his knees would buckle.

Realizing his fists were doubled, his knuckles white, he tried to relax, to shift his thoughts elsewhere. He remembered the day in October when he had met Stella Daniels during the cleanup effort. He thought of their one night together and his desire became a steady flame.

He hoped he would see her on this trip, although since their encounter, he had followed her wishes and refrained from calling her to go out again. The agreement to avoid further contact hadn't stopped him from thinking about her.

At the time he and Stella parted ways, he expected it to be easy. In the seven years since he lost his wife and baby son, women had come and gone in his life, but he had never been close to any of them. Stella had been different because he hadn't been able to walk away and forget her.

He settled in the seat as the plane approached the small Royal airport. Royal was a West Texas town of very wealthy people—yet their wealth hadn't been enough to help them escape the whirlwind.

Almost an hour later he walked into the dining room at the Cozy Inn, his gaze going over the quiet room that was almost empty because of the afternoon hour. He saw the familiar face of Cole Richardson, whose twin, Craig, was one of the storm's fatalities. A woman was seated near Cole. Aaron's heart missed a beat when he saw the brown hair pulled back severely into a bun. He could remember taking down that knot of hair and watching it fall across her bare shoulders, transforming her looks. Stella Daniels was with Cole. Aaron almost whispered "My lucky day" to himself.

Eagerness to see her again quickened his step even though it would get him nowhere with her. He suspected when she decided something, she stuck by her decision and no one could sway her until she was ready to change. Her outfit—white cotton blouse buttoned to her throat and khaki slacks with practical loafers—was as severe and plain as her hairdo. She wore almost no makeup. Few men would look twice at her and he wondered whether she really cared. Watching her, a woman who appeared straitlaced and plain, Aaron couldn't help thinking that the passionate night they'd had almost seemed a figment of his imagination.

As Aaron approached them, Cole stood and Stella glanced over her shoulder. Her gaze met Aaron's and her big blue eyes widened slightly, a look of surprise forming on her face, followed by a slight frown that was gone in a flash.

He reached Cole and held out his hand. "Hi, Cole. Have a seat."

"Aaron, good to see you," Cole said. Looking ready for construction work, he wore one of his T-shirts with the red, white and blue R&N Builders logo printed across the front. "You know Stella Daniels."

Bright, luminous eyes gazed at him as he took her hand in his. Her hand was slender, warm, soft, instantly stirring memories of holding her in his arms.

"Oh, yes," he answered. "Hi, Stella," he said, his voice changing slightly. "We've met, but if we hadn't, anyone who watches television news would recognize you. You're still doing a great job for Royal," he said, and she smiled.

One of the administrative assistants at town hall, Stella had stepped in, taking charge after the storm and trying to help wherever she could. It hadn't taken long for reporters to notice her and start getting her on camera.

Aaron shed his leather jacket and sat across from Cole, aware of Stella to his left. He caught a whiff of the rose-scented perfume she wore, something old-fashioned, but it was uniquely Stella and made him remember holding her close, catching that same scent then.

"I'm glad to have you back in Royal," Cole said. He looked thinner, more solemn, and Aaron was saddened by Cole's loss as well as the losses of so many others in town. He knew from experience how badly it could hurt.

"I know help is needed here, so I'm glad to be back."

"Thanks," Cole said. "I mean it when I say I appreciate that. When you can, drop by the Texas Cattleman's Club. They're rebuilding now and moving along. They'll be glad to have you here, too."

"Our club friends in Dallas said to tell you and the others hello."

Cole nodded as he glanced at Stella. "Getting to the business at hand, Stella and I were talking about areas where more lumber is needed—all over the west side of town, it seems."

"Each time I see Royal, I can't believe the destruction. It still looks incredible. I've made arrangements to get another couple of our work crews here."

"R&N Builders have helped tremendously," Stella said.

"I'm sure everyone in town thanks you for doing such a great job right from the start, Stella—acquiring generators, getting help to people and directing some of the rescue efforts. When disaster happens unexpectedly like that, usually all hell breaks loose and it takes a calm head to help the recovery," Aaron stated.

"Thanks. I just did what I could. So many people pitched in and we appreciate what R&N Builders, plus you and Cole individually, have donated and done to aid Royal."

"We're glad to. Everyone in the company wanted to help," Cole replied. "So we're adding two more work crews. Stella, you can help coordinate where they should go. I asked men to volunteer for the assignment. They'll be paid by us the same as if they were working on a job at home, but R&N is donating their services to help Royal rebuild."

"That would be a tremendous help," Stella said. "Local companies are booked solid for the next few months. There's so much to be done that it's overwhelming."

"Also, we might be able to get one of the wrecking companies we work with to come in here and pick up debris. I doubt you have enough help now when there's so much to clean up," Aaron said.

"We need that desperately. We have some companies from nearby towns, but we can use more help. There is an incredible amount of debris and it keeps growing as they get the downed trees cut up."

Cole made a note on a legal pad in front of him.

"Right now I wonder if we'll ever get all the debris cleared. It would be great to have more trucks here to help haul things away."

Stella made notes as they discussed possibilities for the next hour. Even as he concentrated on the conversation, Aaron could not keep from having a sharp awareness of Stella so nearby. He wished she had not asked him to back off and forget their night of passion.

He'd done so, but now that he was back in her presence, he found it difficult to keep memories from surfacing and wished he could take her out again, dance with her and kiss her, because it had been an exciting, fun night.

Her long slender fingers thumbed through the notebook she held as she turned to a page of figures. He recalled her soft hands trailing across his bare chest, and looked up to meet her blue-eyed gaze.

She drew a deep breath and her cheeks flushed as she looked down and bent over her open binder. Startled, he realized she had memories, too. The idea that she had been recalling that night stirred him and ignited desire. He wondered how many men paid no attention to her because of her buttoned-up blouses and austere appearance. Her actions that night hadn't been austere. Aware he should get his thinking elsewhere, he tried to focus on what Cole was saying.

At half past three Cole leaned back in his chair. "Sorry to have to break this up. You two can continue and, Aaron, you can fill me in later. I'm going out to a long-time friend Henry Markham's ranch to stay five or six days. He invited me out. He also lost his brother in the storm and he's had a lot of damage, so I'm going to help him. I'll see you both next week and we can continue this."

"Don't forget," Stella said, "I have to leave town for part of the day tomorrow. I'll be back in the afternoon." As Cole nodded, she looked at Aaron. "I'm flying to Austin where my sister lives."

"If you need to stay longer, you should," Cole said.

"I don't think I'll need to stay. Just a short time with her and then I'll be back."

Cole glanced at Aaron. "I'm glad you're here, Aaron. We've got good people running the place in Dallas while we're gone, so everything should be all right."

"It'll be fine. George Wandle is in charge. And

if anything comes up he promised he would call one of us."

"Good deal." Cole stood, pulled on a black Western-cut jacket and picked up his broad-brimmed Resistol hat. "Thanks, Stella, for meeting with me."

"All the thanks go to you and Aaron for the help you and your company are giving to Royal. You've been terrific."

"We're glad to help where we can. Aaron, if you need me for anything, I have my phone with me."

"Sure, Cole."

Aaron watched his partner walk through the restaurant and then he turned back to Stella. "It's nice to see you again."

"Thank you. It's nice to see you, too. I really mean it. Your company has done so much to help."

"There's still so much more to do. How's the mayor?"

A slight frown creased her brow as she shook her head at him. "Since the mayor was in the town hall when it sustained a direct hit, he was hurt badly. He was on the critical list a very long time. He's hurt badly with broken bones, internal ruptures and complications after several surgeries.

He was in the ICU for so long. With all the problems he's had, he's still a long way from healed."

"That's tough. Tough for him, for you, for all who work for him and for the town. The deputy mayor's death complicated things even more. No one's really in charge. You've sort of stepped into that void, Stella."

"I'm just doing what I can. There are so many things—from destroyed buildings to lost records and displaced pets. Megan Maguire, the animal shelter director, has worked around the clock a lot of the time. It just takes everybody pulling together and it's nice you're back to help."

He smiled at her. "Maybe, sometime, you need a night out to forget about Royal for a few minutes."

"Frankly, that sounds like paradise, but I don't have time right now. Someone texts or calls every other minute. This has been one of the quietest afternoons, but this morning was a stream of calls."

"Royal could manage without you for a couple of hours."

"Don't tempt me, Aaron," she said, smiling at him. "And I won't be here tomorrow."

"I have the feeling that you're working late into the night, too."

"You're right, but every once in a while now, there'll be a lull in the calls or appointments or hospital visits. Lately, I've had some nights to myself. While you're here, let me show you which projects Cole has finished and where we need the work crews next."

She spread a map on the table and he pulled his chair closer to her. Aware of her only inches away now, he once again inhaled a faint scent of her rose perfume. He helped her smooth the map out and leaned close, trying to focus on what she told him but finding it difficult to keep his attention from wandering to her so close beside him.

She showed him where they had repaired houses and finished building a new house. Stella told him about different areas on the west side of town, which had taken the brunt of the storm, the problems, the shortages of supplies, the people in the hospital. The problems seemed staggering, yet she was quietly helping, as were so many others she told him about.

He wondered if she had suffered some deep loss herself and understood their pain. He wouldn't ask, because she probably wouldn't want to talk about it. He didn't want anyone to ask him about his loss and he hadn't reached a point where he could talk about it with others. He didn't think he ever would. The hurt was deep and personal.

"Aaron?"

Startled, he looked at her. "Sorry, I was thinking about some of these people and their terrible losses. Some things you can't ever get back."

"No," she answered, studying him with a solemn expression. "Houses can be rebuilt, but lives lost are gone. Even some material possessions that hold sentimental value or are antiques—there's no replacing them. You can't replace sixty-year-old or older trees—not until you've planted new ones and let them grow sixty or seventy years. It tears you up sometimes." She smiled at him. "Anyway, I'm glad you're here."

"We'll just help where we can. To have a bed and a roof over your head is good and we need to work toward that for everyone."

"Very good. You and Cole are a godsend," she said, smiling at him and patting his hand.

He placed his hand on hers. Her hand was soft, warm, smooth. He longed to draw her into his arms and his gaze lowered to her mouth as he remembered kissing her before.

She slipped her hand out from under his. "I think they're beginning to set up the dining room for tonight. I wonder if they want us to leave," she said. Her words were slightly breathless and her reaction to him reinforced his determination to spend time with her again.

"We're not in anyone's way and I doubt they want us to leave."

"I didn't realize how long we've talked," she said.

"Have dinner with me. Then I'll give you a ride home tonight."

"I'm still staying here at the inn until the repairs are done on my town house," she said.

"I'm staying here, too, so I'll see you often," he said. She had a faint smile, but he had the feeling that she had put up a barrier. Was she trying to avoid the attraction that had boiled between them the last time they were together? Whatever it was, he wanted to be with her tonight for a time. "Unless you have other plans, since we're both staying here, then, by all means, have dinner with me."

There was a slight hesitation before she nodded. "Thank you," she replied. Even though she accepted his invitation, she had a touch of reluctance in her reply and he had the feeling she was not eager to eat with him.

"Is this headquarters for you?" he asked, his thoughts more on her actions than her words.

"Not at all. I'm not in charge—just another administrative assistant from town hall helping like the others."

"Not quite just another administrative assistant," he said, looking at her big blue eyes and remembering her passionate responses. For one night she had made him forget loss and loneliness. "Should your town house be on our list of places to help with reconstruction?" he asked her.

"Thank you, no. The damage wasn't that extensive, but I was pretty far down on the priorities list. I finally have the work scheduled and some of it has already started. I'm supposed to be back in my place in about a week. Thank goodness. I want to be there before Christmas."

"Good, although I'm glad you're staying here in the hotel because that means we can see each other easily," he said, deciding he would get his suite moved to whatever floor she was on. "They're setting up for tonight and I need to wash up before dinner. Want to meet again in an hour?" he asked her.

"That's a good idea. I've been busy since seven this morning and I'd welcome a chance to freshen up."

As they walked out of the restaurant, he turned to her. "What floor are you on?"

"The sixth floor. I have a suite."

"The same floor I'm on," he said, smiling at her.

"That's quite a coincidence," she said in a skeptical voice.

"It will be when I get my suite moved to the sixth floor, after seeing you to your suite."

She laughed. "I can find my own way to my suite. You go try to finagle a suite on the sixth floor. I don't think you can. It's hopeless. Every available space has been taken because of so many homeless folks having their houses repaired after the storm. People reserved every nook and cranny available in Royal and all the surrounding little towns. Some had to go to Midland, Amarillo and Lubbock. We're packed, so I don't think I'll see you on my floor."

"So you approve if I can get a suite," he said.

"I figure it won't happen," she answered, looking at him intently.

"Not if you don't approve," he said.

"I don't want more complications in my life and you're a wicked influence, Aaron," she said mischievously, for the first time sounding as if she had let down her guard with him.

"Wicked is more fun and you know you agree," he said softly, standing close in front of her. "I'll show you tonight when we're together."

"Oh, no, you won't. I don't need you to show me one thing. We'll have dinner, talk a little and say good-night. That's the agenda. Got it?"

"Oh, I have an agenda. I had it the moment I walked through the door and saw you sitting there with Cole. One of the goals on my agenda is to get you to take down your hair."

"Amazing. One of my goals is to keep my hair pinned up, so one of us is going to fail completely," she said, her blue eyes twinkling.

Eager to be with her for the whole evening, to flirt and dance and hopefully kiss, he leaned a bit closer. "If I placed my hand on your throat, I'll bet I'd feel your pulse is racing. You want the same thing I do. I'm looking forward to dinner and spending the evening together."

"I'm looking forward to the evening, too, so I can talk to you more about how you and your company can continue to help with the restoration of Royal. You're doing a wonderful job so far, and it's heartwarming to know you're willing to continue to help."

"We'll help, but tonight is a time for you to relax and catch your breath. It's a time for fun and friendship and maybe a kiss or two to take your mind off all the problems, so don't bring them with you. C'mon, I'll walk you to your door," he said, taking her arm and heading to the elevators.

She laughed. "Well now, don't *you* have a take-charge personality."

"It gets things done," he answered lightly as they entered the elevator and rode to the sixth floor. When they got off, she walked down the hall and put her key card in a slot. As she opened the door, she held the handle and turned to him.

"Thanks, Aaron. I'll meet you in the lobby."

"How's seven?" he asked, placing one hand on the door frame over her head and leaning close.

"It's good to see you again. I'm looking forward to the evening."

Her eyes flickered and he saw the change as if she had mentally closed a door between them. "Since I'm leaving town tomorrow, let's make it an early evening, because I have to get up at the crack of dawn. My life has changed since you first met me. I have responsibilities now that I didn't have then."

"Sure, whatever you want," he said, wondering what bothered her. For a few minutes downstairs she had let down that guard. He intended to find out why she was now being distant with him. "See you at seven."

"Bye, Aaron," she said, and stepped inside her suite, closing the door.

As he rode down in the elevator, his thoughts were on her. He knew she had regretted their night of lovemaking. It was uncustomary for her and in the cool light of day, it upset her that she had allowed herself to succumb to passion. Was she still suffering guilt about that night?

He didn't think that was what had brought on the cool demeanor at the door of her suite. Maybe partially, but it had to be more than that. But what else could it be? He intended to find out.

He took the elevator back down and crossed the lobby, determined to get a suite on the sixth floor even if he had to pay far more to do so.

It turned out to be easier than he had thought because someone had just moved out.

My lucky day.

Two

Stella Daniels walked through the living room of the suite in the Cozy Inn without seeing her surroundings. Visions came of Aaron when he had strolled to the table where she sat with Cole. Looking even better than she had remembered, Aaron exuded energy. His short dark blond hair in a neat cut added to his authoritative impression. The warmth in his light brown eyes had caused her heart to miss a beat.

She had a mixture of reactions to seeing him—excitement, desire, dread, regret. She hoped she'd managed to hide her tangled opposing emotions as she smiled and greeted him. Her first thought was how handsome he was. Her second was happiness to see him again, immediately followed by wishing he had stayed in Dallas where the company he shared with Cole was headquartered. His presence complicated her busy life more than he knew.

She'd offered her hand in a business handshake, but the moment his fingers had closed over hers, her heartbeat had jumped and awareness of the physical contact had set every nerve quivering. Memories taunted and tempted, memories that she had tried to forget since the one night she had spent with Aaron in October.

It had been a night she yielded to passion—which was so unlike her. Never before had she done such a thing or even been tempted to, but Aaron had swept her away. He had made her forget worries, principles, consequences, all her usual levelheaded caution, and she had rushed into a blissful night of love with him.

Now she was going to pay a price. As time passed after their encounter, she suspected she might have gotten pregnant. Finally she had purchased a pregnancy kit and the results confirmed her suspicions. The next step would be a doctor. Tomorrow she had an appointment in Austin. Her friends thought she was going there to visit her sister; Stella hadn't actually said as much, but people had jumped to that conclusion and she had not corrected anyone. She did not want to see a doctor in Royal who would know her. She didn't want to see one anywhere in the vicinity who would recognize her from her appearances on television since the storm. If a doctor confirmed her pregnancy, she wanted some time to make decisions and deal with the situation herself before everyone in Royal had the news, particularly Aaron.

Tomorrow she would have an expert opinion. Most of the time she still felt she wasn't pregnant, that something else was going on. It had only been one night, and they'd used protection—pregnancy shouldn't have resulted, regardless of test results or a missed period.

She studied herself in the mirror—her figure hadn't changed. She hoped the pregnancy test was wrong, even though common sense said the test was accurate.

Given all that was going on, she should have turned Aaron down tonight, but she just couldn't do it.

She looked at her hair and thought about what

he had said. She would keep it up in a bun as a reminder to stop herself from another night of making love with him. In the meantime, she was going to have dinner with him, work with him and even have fun with him. Harmless fun that would allow them each to say goodbye without emotional ties—just two people who had a good time working together. What harm could there be in that?

Unless it turned out that she was pregnant. Then she couldn't say goodbye.

She showered, took down her hair to redo it and selected a plain pale beige long-sleeved cotton blouse and a dark brown straight wool skirt with practical low-heeled shoes. She brushed, twisted and secured her hair into a bun at the back of her head. She didn't wear makeup. Men usually didn't notice her and she didn't think makeup would make much difference. The times she had worn makeup in high school, boys still hadn't noticed her or wanted to ask her out except when they were looking for help in some course they were taking.

An evening with Aaron. In spite of her promises

to herself and her good intentions, the excitement tingled and added to her eagerness.

When it was time to go meet Aaron, she picked up a small purse that only held necessities, including her card key, wallet and a list of temporary numbers that people were using because of the storm. She wouldn't need a coat because they wouldn't be leaving the Cozy Inn.

When she stepped off the elevator, she saw him. She tried to ignore the faster thump of her heart. In an open-neck pale blue shirt and navy slacks, he looked handsome, neat and important. She thought he stood out in the crowd in the lobby with his dark blond hair, his broad shoulders and his air of authority.

Why did she have such an intense response to him? She had from the first moment she met him. He took her breath away and dazzled her without really doing anything except being himself.

He spotted her and her excitement jumped a notch. She felt locked into gazing into his eyes, eyes the color of caramel. She could barely get her breath; realizing how intensely she reacted to him, she made an effort to break the eye contact.

When she looked again, he was still watching her as he approached.

"You look great. No one would ever guess you've been working since before dawn this morning."

"Thank you," she answered, thinking he was just being polite. Nobody ever told her she looked great or gorgeous, or said things she heard guys say to women. She was accustomed to not catching men's attention so she didn't give it much thought.

"I have a table in the dining room," he said, taking her arm. The room had been transformed since they'd left it. Lights had been turned low, the tables covered in white linen tablecloths. Tiny pots wrapped in red foil and tied with bright green satin bows held dwarf red poinsettias sprinkled with glitter, adding to the festive Christmas atmosphere.

A piano player played softly at one end of the room in front of a tiny dance floor where three couples danced to a familiar Christmas song. Near the piano was a fully decorated Christmas tree with twinkling lights.

Aaron held her chair and then sat across from

her, moving the poinsettia to one side even though they could both see over it.

"I haven't seen many Christmas trees this season," she said. "It's easy to even forget the holiday season is here when so many are hurting and so much is damaged."

"Will you be with your family for Christmas?"

"No. My parents don't pay any attention to Christmas. They're divorced and Christmas was never a fun time at our house because of the anger between them. It was a relief when they finally ended their marriage."

"Sorry. I know we talked about families before. Earlier today you said you are going to see your sister in Austin tomorrow. Do you see her at Christmas?"

"Some years I spend Christmas at her house. Some years I go back and forth between my parents and my sister. Mom has moved to Fort Worth. She's a high school principal there. After the divorce my dad moved his insurance business to Dallas because he had so many customers in the area. I see him some, but not as much as my mom. My grandmother lives with her and my grandfather is deceased."

"So this year what will you do at Christmastime?"

"I plan to stay here and keep trying to help where I can until the afternoon of Christmas Eve. Then I'll fly to Austin to be at my sister's. I have a feeling the holidays will be extremely difficult here for some people. I'm coming back Christmas afternoon and I've asked people here who are alone to come over that evening—just a casual dinner. So far there are about five people coming."

"That's nice, Stella," Aaron said, sounding sincere with a warmth in his gaze that wrapped her in its glow.

"What about you, Aaron? Where will you spend Christmas? You know more about my family than I do about yours."

For an instant he had a shuttered look that made her feel as if she had intruded with her question. Then he shrugged and looked at her. "My parents moved to Paris and I usually go see them during the holidays. My brother is in Dallas and I'll be with him part of the time, although he's going to Paris this year. I like to ski, and some years I ski. This year I'll see if I can help out around here. You're right. A holiday can hurt badly if someone has lost his home or a loved one. After losing his brother, Cole will need my support. So I'm going to spend the holidays in Royal."

As he spoke quietly, there was a glacial look in his eyes that made her feel shut out. She wondered about his past. More and more she realized how little she knew about him.

Their waiter appeared to take their drink order, and Aaron looked at her, his brown eyes warm and friendly again. "The last time we were together you preferred a glass of red wine. Is that what you'd like now?"

She shook her head. "No, thank you. I would prefer a glass of ice water. Maybe later I'll have something else," she said, surprised that he remembered what she had ordered before. She didn't want to drink anything alcoholic and she also didn't care to do anything to cause him to talk about the last time they were together.

"Very well. Water for the lady, please, and I'll have a beer," he said to the waiter.

As soon as they were alone, Aaron turned to her. "Let's dance at least one time and then we'll come back to place our order. Do you already know what you want? I remember last time it was grilled trout, which is also on this menu here."

"I don't know what I want and I need to read the menu. I'll select something and then we'll dance," she said, trying to postpone being in his arms. If she could gracefully skip dancing, she would, but he knew from the last time that she loved to dance. He was remembering that last time together with surprising clarity. She figured he had other women in his life and had forgotten all about her.

"Let's see what we want. When he brings drinks, we can order dinner. I remember how much you like to dance."

"You have a good memory."

"For what interests me," he said, studying her.

"What?" she asked, curious about the intent way he looked at her.

"You're different from last time. Far more serious."

Her breath caught in her throat. "You notice too much, Aaron. It's the storm and all the problems. There are so many things to do. How can I look or feel or even be the same person after the event that has touched each person who lives here," she said, realizing she needed to lighten the situation a bit so he would stop studying her and trying to guess what had changed and what was wrong.

"C'mon. One dance. You need to get your mind off Royal for just a few minutes at least. We can order dinner after a dance. You're not going to faint on the dance floor from hunger. Let it go for a minute, Stella. You've got the burden of the world on your shoulders."

She laughed and shook her head. "I don't think it's that bad. Very well, you win," she said. By trying to stay remote and all-business, she was drawing more attention instead of less, which wasn't what she wanted.

"That's more like it," he said, smiling. "What time do you leave in the morning?" he asked.

"I'll fly the eight-o'clock commuter plane from here to Dallas and change planes for Austin."

They reached the dance floor as the music changed to an old-time fast beat. She was caught in Aaron's direct look as they danced, and his brown eyes had darkened slightly. Desire was evident in his expression. Her insides clenched while memories of making love with him bombarded her.

His hot gaze raked over her and she could barely get her breath. How could she resist him? He was going to interfere in her work in Royal, interfere in her life, stir up trouble and make her want him. The last part scared her. She didn't want Aaron involved too soon because he was a man who was accustomed to taking charge and to having things his way.

Watching him, she gave herself to dancing around the floor with him, to looking into brown eyes that held desire and a promise of kisses, to doing what he said—having fun and forgetting the problems for just a few minutes. The problems wouldn't go away, but she could close her mind to them long enough to dance with Aaron and have a relaxing evening.

As they danced the beat quickened. Smiling, she shut her mind to everything except dancing and music and a drumming beat that seemed to match her heartbeat. The problems would be waiting, but for a few minutes, she pushed them aside.

Her gaze lowered to Aaron's mouth and her own lips parted. Having him close at hand stirred up memories she had been trying to forget. If only she could go back and undo that night with him, to stop short at kissing him.

The dance ended and when a ballad began he held her hand to draw her closer.

"Aaron, I thought we were going to have one dance and then go order dinner," she said, catching her breath.

"I can't resist this. I've been wanting to dance with you and hold you close."

The words thrilled her, scared her and tormented her. They danced together and she was aware of pressing lightly against him and moving in step with him. Memories of being in his arms became more vivid. His aftershave was faint but she recalled it from before. Too many things about him were etched clearly in her memory, which hadn't faded any in spite of her efforts to try to avoid thinking about him.

The minute the song ended, she stepped away and smiled. "Now, we've danced. Let's go order so we get dinner tonight."

"There, that's good to see you relax a little and laugh and smile. That's more the way I remember you."

"I think you just wanted to get your way."

"No. If I just wanted to get my way, we wouldn't be here right now. We'd be upstairs in my room."

She laughed and shook her head, trying to make light of his flirting and pay no attention to it.

At their table she looked over the menu. She selected grilled salmon this time and sipped her cold water while Aaron drank a beer.

"See, it's good to let go of the problems for at least a brief time. You'll be more help to others if you can view things with a fresh perspective."

"I haven't done much of this. The calls for help have been steady although it's not like it was at first. We've had some really good moments when families found each other. That's a triumph and joy everyone can celebrate. And it's touching when pets and owners are reunited. Those are the good moments. Frankly, I'll be ready to have my peace and quiet back."

Her phone dinged and she took it out. "Excuse me," she said as she read the text message and answered it.

Their dinner came and they talked about the houses that were being rebuilt by his company and the families who would eventually occupy them. With Aaron she had a bubbling excitement that

took away her appetite. She didn't want him to notice, so she kept eating small bites slowly. Before
she was half-through, she got a call on her phone.

"Aaron—" She shrugged.

"Take the call. I don't mind."

She talked briefly and then ended the call.
"That's Mildred Payne. She's elderly and lives
alone. Her family lives in Waco. Her best friend
was one of the casualties of the storm. She just
called me because her little dog got out and is
lost. Mildred's crying and phoned me because I've
helped her before. I'm sorry, Aaron, but I have to
go help her find her dog."

He smiled. "Come on. I'll get the waiter and
then I'll take you and we'll find the dog."

"You don't have to."

"I know I don't have to. I want to be with you
and maybe I can help."

"I need to run to my suite and get my coat."

"I'll meet you in the lobby near the front door
in five minutes."

"Thanks."

"Wouldn't miss a dog hunt with you for anything," he said as they parted.

She laughed and rushed to get her coat. When

she came back to the lobby, Aaron was standing by the door. He had on a black leather bomber jacket and once again just the sight of him made her breathless.

His car was waiting outside and a doorman held the door for her as Aaron went around to slide behind the wheel. She told him the address and gave him directions. "You're turning out to be a reliable guy," she said. "I appreciate this."

"You don't know the half about me," he said in an exaggerated drawl, and she smiled.

"To be truthful, I'm glad I don't have to hunt for the dog by myself. I do know the dog. It's a Jack Russell terrier named Dobbin. If you'll stop at a grocery I'll run in and get a bag of treats because he'll come for a doggie treat."

"I'll stop, but if we were home and I was in my own car, we wouldn't have to. My brother has a dog and I keep a bag of treats in the trunk of my car. That dog loves me."

"Well, so do I," she said playfully. "You're willing to hunt for Dobbin."

"When we find Dobbin, we'll go back to the Cozy Inn and I'll show you treats for someone with big blue eyes and long brown hair—"

"Whoa. You just find Dobbin and we'll all be happy," she said, laughing. "Seriously, Aaron, I appreciate you volunteering to help. It's cold and it's dark out. I don't relish hunting for a dog, and Dobbin is playful."

"So am I if you'll give me half a chance," he said. She shook her head.

"I'm not giving you a chance at all. Just concentrate on Dobbin."

"I'll only be a minute," he said, pulling into the brightly lit parking lot of a convenience store. He left the engine running with the heater on while he hurried inside. She watched him come out with a bag of treats.

"Thanks again," she said.

"Hopefully, Dobbin will be back home before we get there. You must get calls for all kinds of problems."

"I'm glad to help when I can. I'm lucky that my house didn't have a lot of damage and I wasn't hurt. Mildred had damage to her house. She's already had a new roof put on and windows replaced. She has a back room that has to be rebuilt, but she was one of the fortunate ones who got help from her insurance company and had a construction company she'd worked with on other jobs, so she called them right after the storm."

"That's the best way. Make the insurance call as soon as possible."

"It worked for Mildred." They drove into a neighborhood that had damage but not the massive destruction that had occurred in the western part of Royal. Houses were older, smaller, set back on tree-filled lots. Stella saw the bright beacon of a porch light. "There's her house where the porch light is on. Mildred is in a block where power got restored within days after the storm. Another help. There she is, waiting for us and probably calling Dobbin."

"He could be miles away. It's a cold night and she's elderly. Get her in where it's warm and I'll drive around looking for Dobbin. Hopefully, he loves treats."

When they reached the house, Aaron turned up the narrow drive. A tall, thin woman with a winter coat pulled around her stood on the porch. She held a sack of dog treats in her hand.

"Thanks again, Aaron. You didn't know what you were in for when you asked me to eat dinner with you. I'll get her settled inside and then

I'll probably walk around the block and look. She said he hadn't been gone long when she called."

"That's good because a dog can cover a lot of ground. I have my phone with me. My number is 555-4378."

"And mine—"

"Is 555-6294," he said, startling her. "I started to call you a couple of times, but you said you wanted to say goodbye, so I didn't call," he said.

That gave her a bigger surprise. She figured he had all but forgotten the night they were together. It was amazing to learn that not only had he thought about calling her, he even knew her phone number from memory. He had wanted to see her again. The discovery made her heart beat faster.

"Stella—"

Startled, she looked around. He had parked and was letting the motor idle. She was so lost in her thoughts, for a moment she had forgotten her surroundings or why they were there. "I'll see about Mildred," she said, stepping out and hurrying to the porch as Aaron backed out of the drive.

"Hi, Mildred. I came as quickly as I could."

"Thank you, Stella. I just knew you would be willing to help."

"I'm with Aaron Nichols, who is Cole Richardson's partner. They own one of the companies that has helped so much in rebuilding Royal. Aaron will drive around to search for Dobbin."

"I appreciate this. He's little and not accustomed to being out at night."

"Don't worry. We'll find him," Stella said, trying to sound positive and cheerful and hoping they could live up to what she promised. "Let's go inside where it's warm and I'll go look, too. You should get in out of the cold."

"You're such a help to everyone and I didn't know who else to turn to. There was George, my neighbor, but their house is gone now and he and his family are living with his sister."

They went inside a warm living room with lights turned on.

"You get comfortable and let us look for Dobbin. Just stay in where it's warm. May I take the bag of treats with me?"

"Of course. Here it is." Mildred wiped her eyes. "It's cold for him to be out." Gray hair framed her long face. She hung her coat in the hall closet and stepped back into the living room.

"I'm going to walk around the block and see if I can find him. Aaron is looking now. We'll be back in a little while."

Mildred nodded and followed Stella to the door.

"This is nice of you, Stella. Dobbin is such company for me. I don't want to lose him."

"Don't worry." She left, closing the door and hurrying down the porch steps. "Dobbin. Here, Dobbin," she called, rattling the treat sack and feeling silly, thinking Dobbin could be out of Royal by now. She prayed he was close and would come home. No one in Royal needed another loss at a time like this.

"Dobbin?" she called, and whistled, walking past Mildred's and the lot next door where a damaged house stood dark and empty. The roof was half-gone and a large elm had fallen on the front porch. Away from the lights the area was grim and cold. She made a mental note to check tomorrow about Mildred's block because she thought this section of town had already had the fallen trees cleared away.

"Dobbin," she called again, her voice sounding eerie in the silent darkness.

A car came around the corner, headlights bright as it drove toward her. The car slowed when it pulled alongside her and she recognized Aaron's rental car. He held up a terrier. Thrilled, she ran toward the car. "You have Dobbin?"

"Dobbin is my buddy now. He's waiting for another treat."

"Hi, Dobbin," she said, petting the dog. "Aaron, you're a miracle man. I'll meet you on Mildred's porch."

"Get in and ride up the drive with me. I'll hold Dobbin so he doesn't escape."

She laughed, thinking it was becoming more and more difficult to try to keep a wall up between them. All afternoon and this evening he had done things to make her appreciate and like him more.

She climbed into the warm car. "I'll hold Dobbin," she said. When Aaron released the terrier, he jumped into her lap. Aaron drove up the drive and parked.

"Come in and meet Mildred because she'll want to thank you."

"Here, you might as well give Mildred the bag of treats. I'll carry Dobbin until we get to the door," Aaron said, taking the dog from her.

On the porch Aaron rang the bell. In seconds the door opened and Mildred smiled. "You found him. Thank you, thank you." She took the dog from Aaron and the bags of treats from Stella. "Please come in. I'm going to put him in my room and I'll be right back. Please have a seat."

When she came back, Stella introduced everyone. "Mildred, this is Aaron Nichols. Aaron, meet Mildred Payne."

"Nice to meet you, ma'am. Dobbin was in the next block, sitting on a porch of a darkened, vacant home as if waiting for a ride home. I had a bag of treats, so he came right to me."

"Good. He doesn't like everybody."

"Mildred, we're going back. It's been a long day and I still have some things to do."

"I wish you could stay. I have cookies and milk."

"Thanks, but we should go," Stella said. Mildred followed them onto the porch, thanking them as they left and still thanking them when they got into the car.

"Now you've done your good deed for today,"

Stella said when he backed down the drive. "It was appreciated."

"It was easy. I think you've become essential to this town."

"No. I'm just happy to help where help is needed. And I'm just one of many helping out. The Texas Cattleman's Club has been particularly helpful, and you and Cole have certainly done more than your fair share."

"Your life may have changed forever because of the storm. I'm surprised you haven't had job offers from people who saw you on television."

"Actually, I have from two places. The attorney general's office in San Angelo has an opening for an administrative assistant and another was a mayor's office in Tyler that has a position that would have the title of office manager."

"Are you interested in either one?"

"No, I thanked them and turned them down. My friends are in Royal and I've grown up here so I want to stay. Besides, they need me here now."

"Amen to that. I'm glad you're staying here because we'll be working together and maybe seeing each other a little more since we're both at the Cozy Inn."

"Did you get your suite changed to the sixth floor?"

"Indeed, I did," he said. "I'll show you."

"I'll take a rain check."

"Oh, well, it's still early. Let's go have a drink and a dance or two."

She hesitated for just a moment, torn between what she should do and what she wanted to do.

"You're having some kind of internal debate, so I'll solve it. You'll come with me and we'll have a drink. There—problem solved. You think you'll be back in Royal tomorrow night?"

"Yes," she said, smiling at him.

When they got back to the hotel, Aaron headed for a booth in the bar. The room was darker and cozier than the dining room. There was a small band playing and a smattering of dancers.

Over a chocolate milk shake, she talked to Aaron. They became enveloped in conversation, first about the town and the storm and then a variety of topics. When he asked her to dance, she put him off until later, relieved that it did not come up again.

"Our Texas Cattleman's Club friends want an

update on the progress here. Cole is good about keeping in touch with both groups."

"I think you'll be surprised by how much they have rebuilt and repaired," she replied.

"Good. I'm anxious to see for myself what's been done."

"You'll be surprised by changes all over town."

Later, she glanced at her watch and saw it was almost one, she picked up her purse. "Aaron, I have to fly out early in the morning. I didn't know it was so late. I never intended to stay this late."

"But you were having such a good time you just couldn't tear yourself away," he teased, and she smiled at him.

"Actually, it has been a good time and the first evening in a while that has had nothing to do with the storm."

They headed out to the elevator and rode to the sixth floor. The hallway was empty and quiet as Aaron walked her to her door.

"Let me take you to the airport in the morning and we can get breakfast there."

"No, thank you. It's way too early."

"I'll be up early. It'll save you trouble and we can talk some more. All good reasons—okay?"

She stopped at her door, getting her card from her purse. "I know you'll get your way in this conversation, too, Aaron. See you in the lobby at six o'clock. Thanks for dinner tonight and a million thanks for finding Dobbin. That made Mildred happy."

"It was fun. Mostly it was fun to be with you and see you again. Before we say good-night, there's something I've been wanting to do since the last time we were together."

"Do I dare ask—what have you been wanting to do?"

"Actually, maybe two or three things," he said softly. "First, I want to kiss you again," he said, moving close and slipping his arm around her waist. Her heart thudded as she looked up at him. She should step back, say no, stop him now, but what harm was there in a kiss? She gazed into his light brown eyes and there was no way to stop. Her heartbeat raced and her lips tingled. She leaned closer and then his mouth covered hers. His arms tightened around her and he pulled her against him.

She wrapped her arms around him to return his kiss, wanting more than kisses. She felt on fire, memories of being in his arms and making love tugging at her.

He leaned over her while he kissed her, his tongue going deep, touching, stroking, building desire. She barely felt his fingers in her hair, but in minutes her hair fell over her shoulders.

She had to stop, to say no. She couldn't have another night like the last one with him.

"Aaron, wait," she whispered.

He looked down at her. His brown eyes had darkened with passion. "I've dreamed of you in my arms, Stella," he whispered. "I want to kiss you and make love."

"Aaron, that night was so unlike me."

"That night was fantastic." He held long strands of her hair in his fingers. "Your hair is pretty."

She shook her head. "I have to go in," she whispered. "Thank you for dinner, and especially for finding the dog."

She opened her door with her card.

"Stella," he said. His voice was hoarse. She paused to look at him.

"I'll meet you in the lobby at six in the morning. I'll take you to the airport."

She nodded. "Thanks," she said, and stepped

into her entryway and closed the door. The lock clicked in place. She rested her forehead against the door and took a deep breath. She didn't intend to get entangled with him at this point in time. Not until she had a definite answer about whether she was pregnant.

At six the next morning Aaron stood waiting. He saw her step off the elevator. She wore a gray coat and a knitted gray scarf around her neck. Her hair was back in a bun. She was plain—men didn't turn to look at her as she walked past, yet she stirred desire in him. She was responsive, quick-witted, kind, helpful, reliable. She was bright and capable and—he knew from firsthand experience—sexy.

He drew a deep breath and tried to focus on other things. But he was already thinking about how long she would be gone and when he would see her again. He hoped that would happen as soon as she returned to Royal. Maybe she would let him pick her up at the airport.

He needed to step back and get a grip. If anyone would be serious in a relationship, it would be Stella. She would want wedding bells, which was reason enough that he should leave her alone. He didn't want a long-term relationship. But she might be one of those women who couldn't deal with a casual affair.

"Good morning," he said as she walked up.

"I'm ready to catch a plane," she said, smiling at him and looking fresh. Beneath the coat he saw a white tailored blouse, tan slacks and brown loafers. Always practical and neat, so what was it about her that made his pulse jump when he saw her?

"You look as if you don't have a care in the world and as if you had a good night's sleep."

"Well, I'm glad I look that way. By the end of some of the days I've spent dealing with all the storm problems, I feel bedraggled."

"I think we can do something about that," he said, flirting with her and wanting to touch her if only just to hold her hand.

"I pass on hearing your suggestions. Let's concentrate on getting to the plane."

"The car is waiting."

As soon as they were headed to the Royal airport, Aaron settled back to drive. "Cole left a list of what we're working on and I have the list we made yesterday of more places where we can help. I'll spend the day visiting the sites, including the Cattleman's Club. When Cole gets back, I want to be able to talk to him about what I can do to help."

"If you have any questions, I'll have my phone, although some of the time it may be turned off."

"I'll manage," he said.

She chuckled. "I'm sure you will."

"You should be able to get away a day without a barrage of phone calls from Royal. Maybe we should think about a weekend away and really give you a break."

She laughed again. "No weekend getaways, Aaron. For more than one reason. You can forget that one. I'll manage without a weekend break."

"Can't blame me for trying," he said, giving her a quick grin. "I'll miss you today," he said.

"No, you won't. You'll be busy. Once people find out who you are and that you're here in Royal, you'll be busy all day long with questions and requests and just listening to problems. I can promise you—get ready to be in high demand."

"Is that the way it's been for Cole? If it has, it probably is good for him because it takes his mind off his loss."

"I'm sure it's what he deals with constantly. We've come a long way, but we still have so far to go to ever recover from all the devastation."

He turned into the small airport and let her out, then parked and came back to join her for breakfast. All too soon she was called to board. He stood watching until she disappeared from sight and then he headed back to town. At least she had agreed to let him pick her up when she returned later today. He was already looking forward to being with her again, something that surprised him. Since losing Paula and Blake, he hadn't been this excited about any woman. Far from it. He felt better staying home by himself than trying to go out with someone and fake having a good time.

That had all changed with Stella—which surprised and puzzled him, because she was so unlike anyone who had ever attracted him before.

Three

Stella left the doctor's office in a daze. The home pregnancy test had been accurate. She was carrying Aaron's baby. Why, oh, why had she gotten into this predicament?

She climbed inside her rental car and locked the doors, relieved to be shut away from everyone else while she tried to adjust to the news.

To make matters worse, now Aaron was not only in Royal, but staying in the neighboring sixth floor suite at the Cozy Inn. He wanted to be with her, to dance with her. She did not want him to know yet. She wished he would go back to Dallas to R&N headquarters and give her time to think things through. She had to decide how much and when she would tell him.

She groaned aloud and put her forehead against the steering wheel. Aaron was a good guy. He had military training, was caring and family oriented, from what little she knew. She could guess his reaction right now. He would instantly propose.

She groaned again and rubbed her temples with her fingertips. "Oh, my," she whispered to the empty car.

She couldn't let Aaron know yet. She would have to get so busy she couldn't go out with him. Her spirits sank lower. He had a suite next to hers—there wasn't going to be any way to avoid him.

He was a take-charge guy and he would definitely want to take charge of her situation.

He would want to marry her. She was as certain of that as she was that she was breathing air and sitting in Austin.

Glancing at her watch, she saw she would be late meeting her sister for lunch. Trying to focus, she started the car and drove to the restaurant they'd agreed on earlier.

At the restaurant, she saw that her sister was already seated. When Stella sat down at the table, her sister's smile faded. "You've had bad news."

"Linda, I just can't believe the truth," Stella said, tears threatening, which was totally unlike her. "I'm pregnant. The test was correct."

"Oh, my, of all people. Stella, I can't believe it. I'll tell you something right now. I know you—you're a wonderful aunt to my children. You're going to love this baby beyond your wildest imaginings. You'll see. I know I'm right."

"That will come, but at the moment this is going to complicate my life. This shouldn't have happened."

"Here comes the waiter."

"I've lost my appetite. There's no way I can eat now."

"Eat something. You'll be sorry later if you don't."

Linda ordered a salad and Stella ordered chicken soup.

As soon as they were alone, Linda turned to Stella. "Look, I'll help any way I can, anytime. When the baby is due, you can stay here and I'll be with you."

"Thank you," Stella said, smiling at her sister. "I can't believe this is happening."

"You've said the dad is a nice guy. Tell him."

"I'll have to think about what I'm going to do first and make some decisions. I know I have to tell him eventually, but not yet. The minute he finds out, I'm sure he'll propose."

"That may solve your problem. Marry him. Accept his proposal. You've already been attracted to each other or you wouldn't be pregnant. There's your solution."

"It's not that simple. Aaron and I are not in love. Look at our parents. That's marriage without love and it was horrible for them and for us. I don't want that. And I feel like there are moments Aaron shuts himself off. He doesn't share much of himself."

"You may be imagining that. Marry him and if he's nice and you've been attracted to each other, you'll probably begin to love him."

"I'm not falling into that trap. Linda, when you married, you and Zane were so in love. That's the way I want it to be if I marry. I couldn't bear to do it otherwise. And it will be a sense of duty for Aaron. He won't give it one second's thought. I'm just sure."

"I'm telling you—if he proposes, marry him. You'll fall in love later."

"Think back to our childhood and the fights that our parents had—the yelling and Mom throwing things and Dad swearing and storming around slamming doors. Oh, no. You can forget the marriage thing. I'll work this out. It's just takes some getting used to and careful planning."

"At least consider what I'm saying. If this man is such a nice guy, that's different from Mom and Dad."

"You know Dad can be a nice guy when he wants to. Mom just goads him. And vice versa. Here comes lunch."

"Try to eat a little. You'll need it."

"It helps to have someone to talk to about it."

"Do you have anyone in Royal?"

"Of course. You should remember Edie. We're close enough that I can talk to her about it. She'll understand, too. Actually, I can probably talk to Lark Taylor."

"I know Lark, but not as well as you do since

you're both the same age. She's not the friendliest person until you get to know her."

"In this storm, believe me, we got to know each other. She and the other nurses from the hospital were out there every day trying to help. So were others that I feel are lifelong friends now. Megan Maguire, the shelter director. I feel much closer to some of the people I've worked with since the tornado. I can talk to them if I want."

"Is he good-looking?"

"I think so."

"Well, then you'll have a good-looking baby."

"Frankly, I hope this baby doesn't look *exactly* like him." Stella smiled. "I'm teasing. I'll think about what you've said. Actually, Aaron is in Royal. I'm having dinner with him tonight."

"There," Linda said, sounding satisfied, as if the whole problem was solved. "Go out with him some before you tell him. Give love a chance to happen. You're obviously attracted to each other."

"I might try, Linda. It's a possibility. But that's enough about me. How are the kids?"

They talked about Linda's three children, their parents, progress in rebuilding Royal and finished their lunch.

As they stood in the sunshine on the sidewalk saying their goodbyes, Linda asked, "You're coming for Christmas, aren't you?"

"Yes. I'll fly in late afternoon Christmas Eve and then back home Christmas afternoon."

"Think about what I've said about marrying the dad. That might turn out a lot better than it did for Mom and Dad."

"I'll think about that one. You take care. See you next time." She turned and hurried to the rental car.

She paused to do a search on her phone and located the nearest bookshop, which was only two blocks away. She drove over and went inside. It took a few minutes to find a book on pregnancy and what to expect with a first baby but before she knew it, she was back in the car, headed to the airport.

All the way to Dallas on the plane she read her new book. She would have to find a doctor in Royal. She was certain Lark could help her there. She knew of two who were popular with women her age.

When she changed planes for Royal, she tucked

her new book into her purse and tossed away the shopping bag in the airport.

As she flew to Royal her dread increased by the minute. She felt as if she had gained ten pounds and her waist had expanded on this trip. She felt uncomfortable in her own skin.

When she stepped off the plane, Aaron was waiting. He had on jeans and a navy sweatshirt. There was no way to stop the warmth that flowed over her at the sight of him and his big smile. She had mixed reactions just as she always had with him.

"Hi," he said, walking up and draping his arm across her shoulders to give her a slight hug as they headed for the main door leading to the parking lot. His brown-eyed gaze swept over her. He saw too much all the time. How long did she have before he could tell she was expecting?

"How's your sister?"

"She's fine. I enjoyed seeing her and all is well."

"Good. I hope you had a restful day."

"I did. How was it here?"

"I imagine if you'd been here, you would answer, 'The usual.' I saw a great deal of the construction and talked to a lot of people. I've been at the Texas Cattleman's Club most of the day. Repairs have begun on the clubhouse. They didn't have total destruction, so it should be done before too long. Actually, I helped some with the work there today." They reached his car and he held the door for her. She watched him walk around the car and slide behind the wheel.

As soon as they were on the freeway, he said, "Let me take you to dinner again. We'll eat at the Cozy Inn if you prefer."

"Thanks, Aaron, I would like that. There's still time for me to go by the hospital this afternoon. By the end of the day, all I'll be up for is the Cozy Inn for dinner. Right now I want to go back to my suite and catch up on emails."

"You may regret doing that. What if you have over a hundred emails waiting? You might have to go look for another lost dog."

She smiled, feeling better.

"I'll tell you one thing," he said, "people are really grateful to you for all you've done. I've had a lot of people out of the blue mention your name. I guess they assume everyone knows who you are and they'll just start talking about 'Stella did this' or 'Stella did that.'"

"I'm always happy to help."

"A lot of people are also talking about Royal needing an acting mayor because it's obvious now that the mayor can't return to work anytime soon. And people I talked to are mentioning your name in the same breath they talk about needing an acting mayor."

"Aaron, I'm an administrative assistant. A lot of us are helping others."

"You've been a big help to lots of people and they appreciate it."

She shook her head and didn't answer him as he pulled to a stop at the front door of the Cozy Inn.

"I'm letting you out here and heading back to the club. I'll see you at seven."

"Let's just meet in the lobby in case I get delayed."

"Sure," he said as a doorman opened her door and she stepped out. She walked into the inn without looking back.

In her room she went straight to her mirror to study her figure. She didn't look one bit different from when she had checked earlier, but she felt different. For one minute she gave herself over to thinking *if only*—if she were married to Aaron this would be one of the most joyous occasions for her.

With a long sigh, she stopped thinking about being married to Aaron and faced the reality that Aaron was in his thirties and still single. She thought back to the night she had met him after the storm. She had been comforting Paige Richardson whose husband, Craig, had died in the tornado. Others had come to call on Paige and someone introduced Stella to Aaron. He was staying in a motel on the edge of Royal, but he offered to take Stella back to the Cozy Inn. They had talked and one thing had led to another until they were in bed together—a rare event to her.

The next morning, when she told Aaron the night was totally uncharacteristic of her and she wanted to avoid further contact, he had agreed to do whatever she wanted and also told her he wasn't in for long-term relationships. She really didn't know much about him. That night they had had fun and lots of laughter, lots of talking, but she was beginning to realize that none of their conversation was about anything serious or important. Last night with him could be described the same way. She knew almost nothing about him and he hadn't questioned her very much about her background. Aaron Nichols would be the father of her child, and it was time she found out more about him. Whether he hated or loved becoming a dad, that was what had happened and they both would have to adjust to the reality of parenthood.

She went to her laptop to read her emails, answering what she needed to, and then left for Royal Memorial Hospital.

The west side of town had taken the brunt of the F4 tornado. Town hall where she had worked was mostly reduced to debris. Almost all three stories of the building had been leveled. The only thing left standing was part of the clock tower—the clock stuck at 4:14 p.m., a permanent reminder of the storm. She couldn't pass it without shivering and getting goose bumps as she recalled the first terrifying moments.

Approaching the hospital, she saw the ripped and shattered west wing. As far as she could tell, rebuilding had not yet begun.

As soon as she went inside the building, outside sounds of traffic and people were shut out. She stepped into an elevator. A nurse had already boarded and Stella realized it was Lark Taylor. They had known each other since childhood, but had become closer in the weeks after the storm. Some accused the ICU nurse of being unfriendly, but Stella couldn't imagine how anyone could feel that way.

"Here to see the mayor's family?" Lark asked.

"Yes. I try to stop by every few days. The changes are slow, but I want to keep up with how he's doing. How's Skye?" As she asked about Lark's sister, Stella gazed into Lark's green eyes and saw her solemn look.

"No change, but thank you for asking about her." Skye had sustained head injuries during the tornado and had been in a medically induced coma ever since. Stella knew Lark was worried about her sister and the baby and it hadn't helped that no one knew who the baby's father was.

"And how's her baby?"

"She's doing well," Lark answered, her voice filling with relief. "I'm so thankful to work here so I can be closer to them."

"I'm glad Skye is doing well," Stella said, happy to hear good news about Skye's tiny baby, who came into the world two months prematurely after her mother was injured during the storm. "Every storm survivor is wonderful," Stella said.

"Right now, we're looking for Jacob Holt." Stella remembered the gossip four years earlier when Jacob had run away with Skye.

"You think he's in Royal?"

"No. If he was here in Royal, I think, in a town this size someone would know. But they're trying to find him. His brother is looking."

"If Keaton doesn't know where Jacob is, I doubt if anyone else does."

"You know so many people—have you heard anything about him?"

"No, nothing. If I do, I'll let you know."

When the elevator stopped on Lark's floor, she stepped into the doorway and turned back.

"If you do hear about him, please let me know. Skye can't tell us anything, and her baby certainly can't. We need to talk to Jacob. With him missing and Skye in a coma, Keaton wants to test the baby's DNA to see if she's a Holt." Lark shook her head. "If you hear anything at all about Jacob, please call me. You have my cell number. Just call or text."

Stella nodded. "I will."

The doors closed and Stella thought about Skye. So many people had been hurt by the storm. But Stella was happy to hear the joy in Lark's voice when she said the little preemie was doing well.

The elevator stopped on Mayor Richard Vance's floor. When she went to the nurse's station, she was told the mayor's wife was in the waiting room.

It was an hour later when Stella left the hospital and hurried to her car. Before she left downtown she stopped at a drugstore to pick up a few things she needed at the Cozy Inn. When she went inside, she recognized the tall, auburn-haired woman she had known for so long because their families were friends. She walked over to say hello to Paige Richardson.

At her greeting Paige turned and briefly smiled. Stella gazed into her friend's gray eyes.

"How are you? How's the Double R, Paige?" she asked about Paige's ranch, which she now had to run without her husband.

"Still picking up the pieces," Paige said. "I heard Aaron Nichols is here again to help. Are you working with Cole and Aaron?"

"A little. A lot of their paperwork comes through

the mayor's office. Cole is out at a friend's ranch now—Henry Markham, who lost his brother, too, in the storm."

"His ranch was badly damaged. Cole's probably helping him."

"The storm was hard on everybody. I'm sure you keep busy with the Double R."

"Some days I'm too busy to think about anything else. Is Cole staying very long with Henry?"

"It should be four or five more days."

"How's the mayor?" Paige asked. "I'm sure you're keeping up with his condition."

"It's a slow healing process, but each time I check, he's holding his own or getting better."

"It's been nice to talk to you because you have some good news. Sometimes I dread coming to town because of more bad news," Paige said.

"This week I've gotten some hopeful reports. It's been great to see you, and you take care of yourself."

"Thanks," Paige replied with another faint smile. "You take care of yourself."

Stella left Paige and greeted other people in the store while she got the things she needed, paid for them and left. Outside she ran into two more people she hadn't seen for a few weeks. They talked briefly and she finally started back to the hotel. Her thoughts shifted from the people she had seen to being with Aaron shortly.

At the Cozy Inn, she walked through to her bedroom and went straight to a mirror to study herself and how she looked. So far, she didn't think she showed no matter which way she stood. She felt fine. The baby should be due next summer. Her baby and Aaron's. She felt weak in the knees whenever she thought about having his baby.

Did she want to go out with him, keep quiet and hope they both fell in love before she had to confess that she was pregnant?

She didn't think that was the way it would work out. She pulled out a navy skirt and a white cotton blouse from the dresser, then put on a navy sweater over the blouse. Once again she brushed and pinned up her hair. She saw she just had a few minutes to get to the lobby to meet Aaron.

If anything, when she spotted him standing near the door of the main restaurant, her excited response resonated deeper than it had the night before. At the same time, she had a curl of apprehension. How would she tell him? When would she? How long could she wait until she did?

Wearing a navy sweater, navy slacks and black cowboy boots, he stood near a potted palm while he waited. She crossed the lobby with its ranch-style plank floor scattered with area rugs. Hotel guests sat in clusters and chatted with each other. The piano music from the restaurant drifted into the lobby. So many local hotels had become temporary homes for the folks displaced by the tornado; whole families were staying and becoming friends.

When she approached, she saw a look in Aaron's brown eyes that made her tingle inside. "I've been looking forward to this all day," he said in greeting.

"So have I," she said. "I haven't had many leisurely dinners with a friend since the storm hit and I hope we can have one tonight."

"We're going to try. You know you can turn that phone off."

She shook her head. "This from the man who would never turn down helping someone. There are too many real emergencies. Later, when everyone calms down and is back on an even keel, I'll think about turning it off, but not yet."

Once they had settled at their table and their drinks arrived—water for her and beer for Aaron—she listened to him describe his work at the Cattleman's Club that day.

"How's your sister?" Aaron asked when he was done.

"She's fine. We had a nice time and had lunch together before I left. We don't see each other much, just the two of us."

"Any change with Mayor Vance?"

She shook her head. "No. But his wife told me he's stable. He's had a very rough time. I talked to Lark Taylor briefly. Her sister Skye is still in a medically induced coma, which sounds terrible to me, but I know it's necessary sometimes. I didn't ask further and, of course, she can't tell me details."

"How is Skye's baby? Still in NICU?"

"Yes, but Lark said Skye's baby is doing well."

"That's good," he said. He tilted his head to look at her. "What?" he asked. "You look puzzled."

"Most single men don't have much to say about a preemie baby in NICU."

He gave her that shuttered look he got occasionally. She seemed to have hit a nerve, but she didn't know why. She didn't pry into other's lives. If Aaron wanted to share something with her, he would.

Their dinners came, and once again her appetite fled even though the baked chicken looked delicious.

About halfway through dinner, Aaron noticed. "No appetite?"

"We had a big lunch just before I went to the airport."

She didn't like looking into his probing brown eyes that saw too much. Aaron was perceptive and an excellent listener, so between the two qualities, he guessed or understood things sooner than some people she had known better and longer.

"One thing I didn't mention," she said, to get his attention off her. "Lark said they were searching for Jacob Holt."

"Cole told me something about that. I imagine they are, with Skye in a coma and a new baby no one knows anything about. It's tough. The Holts must be anxious to know if the child is Jacob's."

"You can't blame him. Most people who've lived here long know about the Holt-Taylor feud."

"From what Cole told me, that feud goes back at least fifty years. What I've always heard is that it was over a land dispute."

"There are other things, too. A creek runs across both ranches, so they've fought over water rights," Stella said.

"There's been enough publicity, even nationally, over the tornado, I'd think Jacob Holt would have heard."

"I can't imagine he's anywhere on earth where he wouldn't hear something about it," she said.

"If the baby is Jacob's, she will be both a Taylor and a Holt and it might diminish the feud."

"High time that old feud died. I wonder if Jacob will ever come back to Royal."

"One more of those mysteries raised by the storm." He smiled at her. "Now speaking of the storm—I have a surprise for you."

Startled, she focused intently on him, unable to imagine what kind of surprise he had.

"I have made arrangements for you to speak to a men's group in Lubbock to raise funds for Royal to help in the rebuilding."

Her surprise increased, along with her dread. "Aaron, thank you for setting up an opportunity to raise funds, but I'm not the one to do it. You didn't even ask me. I'm not a public speaker or the type to talk a group of people into giving money for a cause," she said, feeling a momentary panic.

"You've done this countless times since the storm—you've been the town hall spokesperson really. With Mayor Vance critically ill and Deputy Mayor Rothschild killed in the storm, someone had to step forward and you did. You've done a fantastic job getting people to help out and donate. That's all you've been doing since the storm hit," he said, looking at her intently.

"That's so different," she said, wondering why he couldn't see it. "I did those things in an emergency situation. I was talking to people I knew and it was necessary. Someone had to step in. I was helping, not trying to persuade total strangers to donate to a cause. I'm not the person for that job. I'm not a public speaker and I'm not persuasive. I'm no salesperson or entertainer. A group like that will want to be entertained." Her panic grew because what Aaron expected was something she had never done. "Aaron, I can't persuade people to give money."

"I'm not sure I'm hearing right," he said. "You've persuaded, ordered and convinced people to do all sorts of things since the afternoon the storm hit."

"What I've been doing is so different. I told you, I stepped in when someone had to and the mayor couldn't. Of course people listened to me. They were hurt, desperate—what you've set me up to do is to entertain a group of businessmen in a club that meets once a month with a guest speaker. They're used to a fun speaker and then they go back to work. If I'm to walk in and convince them they should contribute money to Royal, I can't do it." Her old fears of public speaking, of having to try to deal with an audience—those qualms came rushing back.

"When you get there, you'll be fine," he said, as if dismissing her concerns as foolish. "When you meet and talk to them, you'll see they're just like people here. I'll go with you. I think once you start, it'll be just like it is when you're here. Relax, Stella, and be yourself. You've done a great job on national television and state and local news."

He smiled at her and she could tell he didn't have any idea about her limitations.

"When I had interviews that first afternoon and the day after the tornado, I didn't have time to think about being on national television. I just answered questions and went right back to wherever I was needed."

"This isn't going to be different, Stella. You'll see. You'll be great."

"You may be surprised," she said, feeling glum and scared. "Really, Aaron, I don't know why you think I can do this. So when is this taking place?"

"Day after tomorrow. They have a program that day, so you're not the only one to talk to them if that makes you feel better."

"It makes me feel infinitely better. Day after tomorrow. Next time run this past me, please, before you commit me to going."

"Sure. Stella, it never occurred to me that you wouldn't want to do this. It'll be so easy for you. I have great faith in you. This will help raise funds for Royal. People will know you're sincere in what you say, which will help."

She shook her head in exasperation. "That's what keeps me from flat-out telling you I refuse.

I know it will help Royal. I just think someone else might make a better pitch. Thanks, Aaron, but you just don't get it," she said.

"Sure I do and I'm certain it will be easy for you. But all that is in the future. Right now, in our immediate future, I think it's time to dance," he said, holding out his hand.

She went to the dance floor with him, but her thoughts were on the group in Lubbock. She wanted to ask how many people would be in the audience, but she had already made a big issue of it and she couldn't back out now. It was a chance to raise funds and awareness for Royal, so she had to get over her fears and help. She wanted to help her town so maybe she should start planning what to say.

They danced three fast numbers that relaxed her and made her forget the rest of the week. Next, the piano player began an old ballad and Aaron drew her into his arms.

For a moment she relished just being held so close and dancing with him.

They danced one more song and then sat down and talked. Later, he ordered hot cocoa and they talked longer until she looked at her watch and saw it was after one in the morning.

"Aaron, I lost track of time. I do that too much with you. I need to go to my suite. It's been a long day. I'm exhausted," she said as she stood up.

"I'm glad you lost track of time," he said, standing and draping his arm across her shoulders to draw her close to him.

When she reached for her purse, it fell out of her hands. As the purse hit the floor, Aaron bent down instantly to pick it up for her. A coin purse, a small box of business cards and a book fell out.

Horrified, she realized she had not taken the book she had bought earlier out of her purse. She tried to grab it, but Aaron had it in his hand and was staring at the cover with its picture of a smiling baby. For a moment her head spun and she felt as if she would faint, because in his hands that tiny book was about to change their future.

Four

Your Pregnancy and Your First Baby. The title jumped out at Aaron. Stella grabbed the book and dropped it into her purse.

When he looked up at her, all color had drained from her face. She stared, round eyed, looking as if disaster had befallen her.

He felt as if a fist slammed into his chest. Was she pregnant from their night together? She couldn't be, because he'd used protection. Gazing into her eyes, he had his answer that the impossible had happened—apparently the protection they'd used wasn't foolproof after all. Her wide blue eyes looked stricken. Shivering, she clutched her purse in both hands.

"I need to go to my suite," she said in almost a whisper. "We can talk tomorrow."

She brushed past him and for one stunned moment he let her go. Then he realized she would be gone in another minute and went after her. He caught up with her at the elevators and stepped on with her. Another couple joined them and they couldn't talk, so they rode in silence to the fourth floor, where the couple got off.

Aaron looked at her profile. Color had come back into her flushed cheeks. She looked panicked. It had to be because she was carrying his child.

Stunned, he couldn't believe what had happened. She might as well shout at him that he had gotten her pregnant. Her stiff demeanor, terrified expression and averted eyes were solid proof.

He felt as cold as ice, chilled to the bone, while his gaze raked over her. Her sweater hid her waist, but he had seen her waist yesterday and she was as tiny as ever, her stomach as flat as when they had met.

He took a deep breath and followed her out of the elevator.

At her door she turned to face him. "Thank you for dinner. Can we talk tomorrow?"

"Are you really going to go into your suite, get in bed and go to sleep right now?" he asked. His own head spun with the discovery, which explained why she had been so cool the other day when she had first seen him again. Shock hit him in waves and just wouldn't stop. She was pregnant with his baby. He would be a father. He had no choice now in the situation. He had made his choice the night he seduced her and he couldn't undo it now. "You're not going in there and going to sleep."

She met his gaze. "No, I guess I'm not," she replied in a whisper. "Come in."

There was only one thing for him to do. She carried his baby. He had gotten her pregnant. He had taken precautions and both of them thought they had been safe when in reality they had not been. It was done and could not be undone. As far as he could see there was no question about what he needed to do.

She unlocked her door and he closed and locked it behind them, following her into a spacious living area with beige-and-white decor that was similar to the suite he had. The entire inn had a homey appearance with maple furniture, old-fashioned pictures, needlepoint-covered throw pillows, rocking chairs in the living areas and fireplaces with gas logs.

"Have a seat, please. Do you want anything to drink?" she asked.

"Oh, yeah. Have any whiskey?"

"No. There's a bottle of wine," she replied, her voice cold and grim.

"That's okay. I'll pass. Have you been to a doctor yet?"

"Yes. That's where I went today," she said, her voice barely above a whisper. "I couldn't go to a doctor here in Royal where I know everybody and they know me. If they don't know me, a lot of people recognize me now from seeing me on television."

She sat perched on the edge of a wing chair that seemed to dwarf her. He studied her in silence and she gazed back. Her hands were knotted together, her knuckles white; once again she had lost her color. He suspected if he touched her she would be ice-cold.

He was in such shock he couldn't even think.

This was the last possible thing he thought would happen to him. Actually, he'd thought it was impossible.

"You're certain you're pregnant?"

"Yes, Aaron, I am. There isn't really much to talk about right now. It's probably best you think about it before you start talking to me. I know this is a shock."

He stared at her. She was right in that he needed to think, to adjust to what had happened. It was a huge upheaval, bigger even than the storm, where he had merely come in afterward to try to help. Now he had his own storm in his life and he wondered if he could ever pick up the pieces.

She looked determined. Her chin was tilted up and she had a defiant gleam in her eyes. He realized he had been entirely focused on himself and the shock of discovering that he would be a father. He needed to consider Stella.

He crossed the room and pulled her to her feet, wrapping his arms around her. She stood stiffly in his embrace and gazed up at him.

"Stella, one thing I don't have to think about— I'm here for you. I know it's going to be hard, but let's try to reason this out and avoid worry. First, you're not alone. I want—"

She placed her finger on his lips. "Do not make any kind of commitment tonight. Not even a tiny one. You've had a shock, just as I had, and it takes a bit of time to adjust to this. Don't do something foolish on the spur of the moment. Don't do something foolish because of honor. I know you're a man of honor—Cole has said that and he knows you well. It shows, too, in things you've done to help the people here."

"You've had a head start on thinking about this and the future," he said, listening to her speech. "Stella, I don't have to think about this all night. It seems pretty simple and straightforward. We were drawn to each other enough for a baby to happen."

He took her cold hands in his. Her icy hands indicated her feelings and he wanted to reassure her. He saw no choice here.

"Stella, this is my responsibility. I want to marry you."

She closed her eyes for a moment as if he had given her terrible news. When she opened them to look up at him, she shook her head.

"Thank you, but no, we will not get married. I didn't want you to know until I decided what I would do. I knew you would propose the minute you learned about my pregnancy."

"I don't see anything wrong with that. Some women would be happy to get a proposal," he said, wondering if she was thinking this through. "I'm not exactly repulsive to you or poor husband material, am I?"

"Don't be absurd. There's something huge that's wrong with proposing tonight—within the hour you've discovered you'll be a father. We're not in love, Aaron. Neither one of us has ever said 'I love you' to the other."

"That doesn't mean we can't fall in love."

She frowned and her lips firmed as she stared at him and shook her head. "There was no love between my parents. I don't think there ever was," she said. "They had the most miserable, awful marriage. There was no physical abuse or anything like that. There were just tantrums, constant bickering, tearing each other down verbally. My sister and I grew up in a tense, unhappy household. I don't ever want to be in that situation. I'll have to be wildly in love to marry someone. My sister and her husband are, and it's a joy to be around them. They love each other and have a happy family. I couldn't bear a marriage without love and I don't want you to be in that situation, either. We're not in love. We barely know each other. We'll work this out, but marriage isn't the way."

He pulled her close against him to hold her while they stood there quietly. "Look, Stella, we're not your parents. I can't imagine either one of us treating the other person in such a manner."

She stood stiffly in his arms and he felt he couldn't reach her. He'd had his second shock when she turned down his offer of marriage. It didn't occur to him that she wouldn't marry him. Now there were two shocks tonight that hit him and left him reeling.

"You got pregnant when we were together in October," he said.

"Yes," she whispered.

He tilted her face up to look into her eyes. He caressed her throat, letting his fingers drift down her cheek and around to her nape. He felt the moment she relaxed against him. The stiffness left her and he heard her soft sigh.

"I didn't want you to know yet," she whispered.

"Maybe it's best I do. We'll work through this together," he said.

As he looked into her wide blue eyes, he became more aware of her soft curves pressed against him. His gaze lowered to her lips and his heart beat faster as desire kindled.

"Stella," he whispered, leaning closer. When his lips brushed hers, she closed her eyes.

He wrapped his arms more tightly around her, pulling her closer against him as he kissed her. It started as a tender kiss of reassurance. But then his mouth pressed more firmly against hers as his kiss became passionate. He wound his fingers in the bun at the back of her head and combed it out, letting the pins fall.

He wanted her. As far as he was concerned, their problem had a solution and it would only be a matter of time until she would see it. The moment that thought came to him, he remembered her strength in tough situations. If she said no to him, she might mean it and stick by it no matter what else happened.

She opened her eyes, stepping back. "Aaron, when we make love, I want it to be out of joy, not because of worry and concerns. Tonight's not the night."

Her hair had partially spilled over her shoulders and hung halfway down her back. A few strands were still caught up behind her head. Her lips had reddened from his kisses. Her disheveled appearance appealed to him and he wanted to draw her back into his embrace. Instead, he rested his hands lightly on her shoulders.

"You don't have to be burdened with worry and concerns tonight," he said. "We're in this together."

"Aaron, has anything ever set you back in your life?"

Her question was like a blow to his heart. She still hadn't heard about Paula and Blake, and he still didn't want to talk about them or his loss. Over the years, the pain had dulled, but it would never go away. Everyone had setbacks in life. Why would she think he had never had any? "All right, Stella. You want to be alone. I'll leave you alone," he said, turning to go. He had tried to do the right thing and been rebuffed for it.

"Aaron," she said, catching up with him, "I know you're trying to help me. I appreciate it. A lot of men would not have proposed. You're one of the good guys."

Realizing she needed time to think things through, he gazed at her. "I'm the dad. I'm not proposing just for your sake. It's for mine, too. Stella, this baby coming into my life is a gift, not an obligation," he said.

Her eyes widened with a startled expression and he realized she hadn't looked at it from his perspective, other than to expect him to propose.

"We can do better than this," he said, pulling her into his arms to kiss her again, passionately determined to get past her worries and fears.

For only a few seconds she stood stiffly in his arms and then she wrapped her arms around him, pressing against him and kissing him back until he felt she was more herself again and their problems were falling into a better perspective.

As their kiss deepened, his temperature jumped. He forgot everything except Stella in his arms while desire blazed hotly.

Leaning back slightly, he caressed her throat, his hands sliding down over her cotton blouse. He didn't think she could even feel his touch through the blouse, but she took a deep breath and her eyes closed as she held his forearms. Her reaction made him want to peel away the blouse, but he was certain she would stop him. He slipped his hand to the top button while he caressed her with his other hand. As he twisted the button free, she clutched his wrist.

"Wait, Aaron," she whispered.

He kissed away her protest, which had sounded faint and halfhearted anyway. He ran his fingers through her hair, combing it out, feeling more pins falling as the locks tumbled down her back.

"You look pretty with your hair down," he whispered.

She turned, maybe to answer. Instead, he kissed her and stopped any conversation.

"I want to love you all night. I will soon, Stella. I want to kiss and hold you," he whispered when the kiss subsided.

She moaned softly as he twisted free another button, his hand sliding beneath her blouse to cup her breast.

She gasped, kissing him, clinging to him. He wanted to pick her up, carry her to bed, but he suspected she would end their kisses and tell him good-night.

She finally stepped back. "We were headed to the door."

He combed long strands of brown hair from her face. "I'll go, but sometime soon, you'll want me to stay. I'll see you in the morning." He started out the door and turned back. "Don't worry. If you can't sleep, call me and we'll talk."

She smiled. "Thanks, Aaron. Thanks for being you."

He studied her, wondering about her feelings, wondering where they were headed, because he could imagine her sticking to the decisions she had already made involving their future. "Just don't forget I'm half the parent equation."

"I couldn't possibly forget," she said, standing in the open doorway with him.

"Good night," he said, brushing a light kiss on her lips and going to his suite.

When he got there, he went straight to the kitchen and poured himself a glass of whiskey. Setting the bottle and his drink on the kitchen table, he pulled out his billfold. As he sat, he took a long drink. He opened the wallet and looked at a picture of Paula holding Blake. Aaron's insides knotted.

"I love you," he whispered. "I miss you. I'm going to be a dad again. I never thought that would happen. It doesn't take away one bit of love from either of you. That's the thing about love—there's always more."

He felt the dull pain that had been a part of him since losing Paula and Blake. "This isn't the way it was supposed to be. I know, if you were here, you'd tell me to snap out of it, to marry her and be the best dad possible." He paused a moment and stared at the photo. "Paula, Blake, I love you both. I miss you."

He dropped his billfold and put his head in his hands, closing his eyes tightly against the hurt. He got a grip on his emotions, wiped his eyes and took a deep breath. He was going to be a dad again. In spite of all the tangled emotions and Stella's rejection of his proposal, he felt a kernel of excitement. He would be a dad—it was a small miracle. A second baby of his own. How would he ever persuade Stella to marry him? She wanted love and marriage.

He could give her marriage. He would have to try to persuade her to settle for that. Just marriage. A lot of women would jump at such a chance. One corner of his mouth lifted in a grin and he held up his drink in a toast to an imaginary companion. "Here's to you, Stella, on sticking to your convictions and placing a premium on old-fashioned love. You'll be a good mother for our child."

So far, in working with her, Stella had proved to be levelheaded, practical and very intelligent. That gave him hope.

He finished his drink and poured one more, capping the bottle. Then he stood up and put it away. He started to pocket his billfold, but he paused to open it and look once more at the picture of his baby son. As always, he felt a hollow emptiness, as if his insides had been ripped out. Now he was going to have another baby—another little child, his child. It was a miracle to him, thrilling.

Stella had to let him be a part of his child's life. It was a chance to be a dad again, to have a little one, a son or daughter to raise. In that moment, he cared. He wanted Stella to marry him or let him into the life of his child in some way. He wasn't giving up a second child of his. One loss was too many. He sure as hell didn't plan to lose the second baby. He would have to court Stella until she just couldn't say no. He had to try to win her love.

As much as he hurt, he still had to smile. Stella wouldn't go for any insincere attempt to fake love or conjure it up where it didn't exist.

He had to make her fall in love with him and that might not be so easy when he didn't know whether he could ever really love her in return.

The next morning Stella was supposed to have breakfast with Aaron, but he called and told her to go ahead because he'd be late. A few minutes after she'd settled in and ordered, she watched him cross the dining room to her table. He was dressed for a day of helping the cleanup effort in jeans, an R&N sweatshirt and cowboy boots. Even in the ordinary clothes, he looked handsome and her heart began racing at her first glimpse of him. The father of her baby. She was beginning to adjust to the idea of being pregnant even though she had slept little last night.

"Sorry. You shouldn't have waited. Did you order from the menu or are you going with the buffet?"

"I've ordered from the menu and I didn't wait," she said, smiling.

"I'll get the buffet and be right back."

While they ate, Aaron sipped his coffee. "So, did you sleep well last night?" he asked.

"Fine," she replied, taking a dainty bite of yellow pineapple.

"Shall I try again? Did you get any sleep last night?"

She stared at him. "How do you know I didn't?"

"You're a scrupulously honest person so prevarication isn't like you. You were a little too upset to sleep well."

"If you must know, I didn't sleep well. Did you?"

"Actually, pretty good after I thought things through."

"I'm glad. By the way, today after work, I'll try to get something together for the presentation in Lubbock tomorrow. Please tell me this is a small group."

"This is a small group," he said, echoing her words.

She wasn't convinced. "Aaron, is this a large or small group?"

"It's what I'd call in-between."

"That's a real help," she said. He grinned and took her hand in his to squeeze it lightly.

"All you need is an opening line and a closing

line. You know the stuff in between. You'll be fine. I know what I'm talking about. And so will you, so just relax," he said, his eyes warm and friendly. She would be glad to have his support for the afternoon.

When they finished breakfast and stood to go, she caught him studying her waist. She wore a tan skirt and matching blouse that was tucked in. She knew from looking intently in her mirror before she came down for breakfast, that her pregnancy still didn't show in her waist and that her stomach was as flat as ever.

His gaze flew up to meet hers. "You don't look it," he said quietly.

"Not yet. I will," she replied, and he nodded.

They walked out together and climbed into Aaron's car. He dropped her off at the temporary headquarters for town hall and drove away to go to the Cattleman's Club. Today she would be overseeing the effort to sort records that had been scattered by the storm. She wondered how many months—or worse, years—of vital records they would find. She hoped no one's life changed for the worse because of these lost records.

Stella entered the makeshift office that had been

set up for recovered documents. The room held long tables covered with boxes labeled for various types of documents. As Stella put her purse away, Polly Hadley appeared with a box filled with papers that she placed on a cleared space on a desk.

"Good morning, Stella. You're just in time," her fellow administrative assistant said. "Here's another box of papers to sort through. I glanced at a few of these when I found them. What I saw was important," Polly said.

"I'm thankful for each record we find."

"Most of these papers were beneath part of a stockade fence."

"Heaven knows where the fence came from," Stella said.

"I don't want to think about how long we'll be searching for files, papers, records. Some of these were never stored electronically."

"Some records that were stored electronically are destroyed now," Stella stated as she pulled the box closer. "We'll just do the best we can. Thank goodness so many people are helping us."

"I'll be back with more." Polly smiled as she left the makeshift office.

Stella picked up a smudged stack of stapled papers from the top of the pile and looked at them, sighing when she saw they were adoption papers. A chill slithered down her spine as she thought again of important documents they might not ever find. She smoothed the wrinkled papers and placed them in a box of other papers relating to adoptions. She picked up the next set of papers and brushed away smudges of dirt as she read, her thoughts momentarily jumping back to breakfast with Aaron. In some ways it was a relief to have him know the truth. If only he would give her room to make decisions—that was a big worry. As for dinner with him tonight—she just hoped he didn't persist about marriage.

That evening as they ate, she made plans with Aaron to go to Lubbock the next day. She tried to be positive about it, but she had butterflies in her stomach just thinking about it.

She had finished eating and sat talking to Aaron while he sipped a beer when her phone rang. She listened to the caller, then stood up and gave instructions. When she hung up, she turned to Aaron.

"I heard some of that call. Your part," he said.

"We can talk as we walk to the car. That was Leonard Sherman. He's fallen and his daughter is out of town. He can't get up and he needs someone to help him. He hit his head. I told him that I would call an ambulance."

Aaron waited quietly while she made the call. As soon as she finished, she turned to him. "I need to go to his house to lock up for him when the ambulance picks him up. He lives alone near his daughter. He said his neighbor isn't home, either."

"Does everyone in town call you when they have an emergency?"

Smiling, she shook her head. "Of course not, but some of these people have gotten so they feel we're friends and I'll help, which I'm glad to do. It's nice they feel that way. I'm happy to help when I can."

"I'll take you."

A valet brought Aaron's car to the door of the inn. As they drove away, she finished making her calls.

"You don't need to speed," she said. "I don't think he's hurt badly."

"You wanted to get there before they took him in the ambulance, so we will."

In minutes Aaron pulled into Leonard Sherman's driveway. She stepped out of the car and hurried inside while Aaron locked up and followed.

The ambulance arrived only minutes later and soon they had their patient loaded into the back and ready to go to the hospital. As the paramedics carefully pulled away from the curb, Stella locked up Leonard's house, pocketed the key and walked back to the car with Aaron.

"You don't have to go to the hospital with me. I'll call his daughter and she'll probably want to talk to the doctor. He said she's coming back tonight, so hopefully, she'll be home soon."

"I'll go with you. These evenings are getting interesting."

She laughed. "I told you that you don't have to come."

"You amaze me," Aaron said. "I've never told you any news I get about anyone in Royal that you don't already know. People tell you everything. I'll bet you know all sorts of secrets."

"I'm just friendly and interested."

"People trust you and you're a good listener. They call you for help. Mayor Vance doesn't do all this."

Stella watched him drive, thinking he was one person who didn't tell her everything. She always had a feeling that Aaron held personal things back. There were parts of his life closed to her. A lot of parts. She still knew little about him. She suspected Cole knew much more.

She called Leonard's daughter and, to her relief, heard her answer.

When Stella was done with the call, she turned to Aaron. "I'll go to Memorial Hospital to give her the key to his house, but his daughter is back and she'll be at the hospital, so we don't need to stay."

"Good. You said you wanted to get ready for tomorrow, so now you'll have a chance unless calamity befalls someone else in this town to-night."

"It's not that bad," she said.

"I had other plans for us this evening. We're incredibly off the mark."

"That's probably for the better, Aaron," she said.

"You don't have to do everything for everyone. Learn to delegate, Stella."

"Some things are too personal to delegate. People are frightened and hurting still. I'm happy to help however I can if it makes things even the smallest bit better."

He squeezed her hand. "Remind me to keep you around for emergencies," he said lightly, but she again wondered about what he kept bottled up and how he had been hurt. He might want them to be alone tonight, but she had to respond when someone called.

And she stuck to her guns. When they got back to the hotel, she told Aaron good-night early in the evening so she could get ready to leave for Lubbock with him the next morning.

As soon as she was alone in her suite, she went over her notes for the next day, but her thoughts kept jumping to Aaron. Every hour they spent together bound her a little more to him, making his friendship a bit more important to her. Now she was counting on him for moral support tomorrow.

The next morning, when she went to the lobby to meet Aaron and head for Lubbock, she saw him the minute she emerged from the elevator. The sight of him in a flawless navy suit with a red tie took her breath away and made her forget her worries about speaking. He looked incredibly handsome, so handsome, she wondered what he saw in her. She was plain from head to toe. Plain clothes, plain hair, no makeup. This handsome man wanted to marry her and she had turned him down. Her insides fluttered and a cold fear gripped her. Was she willing to let him go and marry someone else? The answer still came up the same. She couldn't marry without love. Yet Aaron was special, so she hoped she wasn't making a big mistake

This baby coming into my life is a gift, not an obligation. She remembered his words from the night before last. How many single men who had just been surprised to learn they would be a dad would have that attitude? Was she rejecting a very special man?

He saw her and she smiled, resisting the temptation to raise her hand to smooth her hair.

She was aware of her plain brown suit, her skirt ending midcalf. She wore a tan blouse with a round neck beneath her jacket. Her low-heeled brown pumps were practical and her hair was in its usual bun. When she crossed the lobby, no heads would turn, but she didn't mind because it had been that way all her life.

When she walked up to him, he took her arm. "The car is waiting," he said. "You look pretty."

"Thank you. Sometimes I wonder if you need to get your eyes checked."

He smiled. "The last time I was tested in the air force, I had excellent eyesight," he remarked. "You sell yourself short, Stella. Both on giving this talk and on how you look."

She didn't tell him that men rarely told her she was pretty. They thanked her for her help or asked her about their problems, just as boys had in school, but they didn't tell her how pretty she looked.

In minutes they were on the highway. She pulled out a notebook and a small stack of cards wrapped with a rubber band. "These are my notes. I have a slide presentation. I think the pictures may speak for themselves. People are stunned when they see these."

When she walked into the private meeting room in a country club, her knees felt weak and the butterflies in her stomach changed to ice. The room was filled with men and women in business suits—mostly men. It was a business club and she couldn't imagine talking to them. She glanced at Aaron.

"Aaron, I can't do this."

"Of course you can. Here comes Boyce Johnson, my friend who is president," he said, and she saw a smiling, brown-haired man approaching them. He extended his hand to Aaron, who made introductions that she didn't even hear as she smiled and went through the motions.

All too soon, Boyce called the group to order and someone made an introduction that Aaron must have written, telling about how she had helped after the storm hit Royal. And then she was left facing the forty or so people who filled the room, all looking at her and waiting for her to begin.

Smiling and hoping his presence would reassure her, Aaron sat listening to Stella make her presentation, showing pictures of the devastation in the first few hours after the storm hit Royal. That alone would make people want to contribute. After her slide presentation, Stella talked. She was nervous and it showed. He realized that right after the storm, adrenaline—and the sheer necessity for someone to take charge with Mayor Vance critically injured and the deputy mayor killed—had kept her going. Now that life in Royal was beginning to settle back into a routine, she could do it again, but she had to have faith in herself.

He thought of contacts he had and realized he could help her raise funds for the town. Her slide presentation had been excellent, touching, awesome in showing the storm's fury and giving the facts about the F4 tornado.

He sat looking at her as she talked and realized she might like a makeover in a Dallas salon. She could catch people's attention more. The men today were polite and attentive and she was giving facts that would hold their interest, but if she had a makeover, she might do even better. It should bolster her self-confidence.

She had done interviews and brief appearances almost since the day of the storm. Maybe it was time she had some help. He had statewide contacts, people in Dallas who were good about contributing to worthwhile causes. While she talked, he sent a text to a Dallas Texas Cattleman's Club member. In minutes he got a reply.

He sent a text to a Dallas salon, and shortly after, had an appointment for her.

He hoped she wouldn't balk at changing her hair. She clung to having it up in a bun almost as if she wanted to fade into the background, but hopefully, the makeover in the salon might cause her to be willing to change.

When she finished her speech and opened up the floor to questions, she seemed more poised and relaxed. She gave accurate facts and figures and did a good job of conveying the situation in Royal. Finally, there were no more questions. Boyce thanked her and Aaron for coming. He asked if anyone would like to make a motion to give a check to Stella to take back to Royal now because they seemed to need help as soon as they could possibly get it.

Boyce turned to ask their treasurer how much they had available in their treasury at present and was told there was $6,000.

One of the women made a motion immediately to donate $5,000. It was seconded and passed. A man stood and said he would like to contribute $1,000 in addition to the money from the treasury.

Aaron felt a flash of satisfaction, happy that

they could take these donations back to Royal and happy that he had proved to Stella she could get out and lead the recovery effort now, just as she had right after the storm.

By the time the meeting was over, they had several checks totaling $12,000. Stella's cheeks were once again rosy and a sparkle was back in her blue eyes and he felt a warm glow inside because she was happy over the results.

With the help he planned to give her, he expected her to do even better. As he waited while people still talked to her, he received a text from the TCC member he had contacted. Smiling, he read the text swiftly and saw that his friend had made some contacts and it looked hopeful for an interview on a Fort Worth television station. Aaron sent a quick thank-you, hoping if it worked out Stella would accept.

It was almost four when they finally said goodbye and went to his car. When he sat behind the wheel, he turned to her, taking her into his arms. His mouth came down on hers as he kissed her thoroughly. Finally he leaned away a fraction to look at her.

"You did a great job. See, you can do this.

You've raised $12,000 for Royal. That's fantastic, Stella."

She smiled. "My knees were shaking. Thank heavens you were there and I could look at your smiling face. They were nice and generous. I couldn't believe they would take all that out of their treasury and donate it at Christmastime."

"It's a Christmas present for Royal, thanks to you. That's what that club does. It's usually to help Lubbock, but Royal is a Texas town that is in desperate need of help. You did a great job and I think I can help you do an even bigger and better one," he said.

She laughed. "Aaron, please don't set me up to talk to another group of businesspeople. I'm an administrative assistant, not the mayor."

"You did fine today and I promise you, I think I can help you do a bit better if you'll let me."

"Of course, I'll let you, but I keep telling you, this is not my deal."

"You're taking $12,000 back to Royal. I think you can make a lot more and help people so much."

"When you put it that way—what do you have in mind?"

"I have lots of contacts in Dallas and across the state. Let me set up some meetings. Not necessarily a group thing like today—what I have in mind is meeting one-on-one or with just two or three company heads who might make some big donations. You can also make presentations to agencies that would be good contacts and can help even more."

"All right."

"Good. After your talk today I went ahead and contacted a close friend in Dallas. Through him you may get a brief interview on a local TV show in Fort Worth. Can I say you'll do it?"

"Yes," she answered, laughing. "You're taking charge again, Aaron."

"Also, if you'll let me contact them, I think I can get meetings in Dallas with oil and gas and TV executives, as well as some storm recovery experts. The television people will help get out the message that Royal needs help. The oil and gas people may actually make monetary donations. How's that sound?"

"Terrifying," she said, and smiled. "Well, maybe not so bad."

"So I can try to set up the meetings with the various executives?"

She stared at him a moment while she seemed to give thought to his question. "Yes. We need all the help we can get for the people at home."

"Good," he said, kissing her lightly.

"Let's take some time and talk about dealing with the press and interviews. We can talk over dinner. The press is important."

"I'll be happy to talk about interviews, but I don't think that I'll be giving many more."

"It's better to be ready just in case," he said, gazing into her wide blue eyes.

"Also I sent a text and asked for a salon make-over in Dallas for you. It's a very nice salon that will really pamper you. Would you object to that?" he asked, thinking he had never known a woman before that would have had to be given a sales pitch to get her to consent to a day at an exclusive Dallas salon.

She laughed. "Aaron, that seems ridiculous. I'm not going into show business. Mercy me. I don't think I need to go to Dallas to have a makeover and then return to Royal to help clean up debris and hunt through rubble for lost documents at town hall. That seems ridiculous."

"Stella, we can raise some money for Royal. A lot more than you did today. Trust me on this," he said, holding back a grin. "I told you that it's a very nice salon."

Shaking her head, she laughed again. "All right, Aaron. I can arrange to get away to go to Dallas. When is this makeover?"

"Someone canceled and they have an opening next Wednesday and I told them to hold it. Or they can take you in January. With the holidays coming, they're booked."

"How long does this take? I'll have to get to Dallas," she said, sounding as if he had asked her to do a task she really didn't relish.

"Cole and I have a company plane. We can fly to Dallas early Tuesday morning and be there in time for you to spend the day. I'll get you to the Fort Worth interview and I'll try to set up a dinner in Dallas that night. Afterward, we can stay at my house. I have lots of room and you can have your own suite there."

She smiled at him. "Very well. I can go to the

salon Wednesday and get this over with. Thank you, Aaron," she said politely.

"Good deal," he said, amused at the reluctance clearly in her voice. "Take a dress along to go out to dinner. The next convenient stop, I'm pulling over to text the salon about Wednesday."

"I think this is going to be expensive for you and a waste of your money. People can't change in a few hours with a makeover. I really don't expect to do many more appearances or interviews."

"Just wait and see," he said.

"While we're on the subject of doing something for Royal, I've been thinking about Christmas. There are so many people who lost everything. We've talked about Christmas being tough for some of them. I want to organize a Christmas drive to get gifts for those who lost their homes or have no income because of their business losses. I want to make sure all the little children in those families have presents."

"That's a great idea, Stella. I'll help any way I can."

"I'm sure others will help. I'll call some of the women I know and get this started. It's late—we should have started before now, but it's not too late to do this."

"Not at all. I think everyone will pitch in on this one. You're doing a great job for Royal."

"Thanks, Aaron. I'd feel better knowing that everyone has presents. We have a list now of all those who were hurt in some way by the storm. It's fairly detailed, so we know who lost homes and who is in the hospital and who lost loved ones or pets—all that sort of thing, and I can use it to compile a list for the Christmas gifts."

With a quick glance he reached over to take her hand. As he looked back at the highway, he squeezed her hand lightly. "Royal is lucky to have you," he said.

She laughed. "And you. And Cole and Lark and Megan and so many other people who are helping." He signaled a turn. "There's a farm road. We're stopping so I can send the text."

As soon as he stopped he unbuckled his seat belt and reached over to wrap his arms around her and pull her toward him.

"Aaron, what are you doing?"

"Kissing you. I think you're great, Stella," he said. As she started to reply, his mouth covered hers. It was as if he had waited years to kiss her. Startled, she didn't move for a second. Then she wrapped her arm around his neck to hold him while she kissed him in return.

What started out fun and rewarding changed as their desire blossomed. She wound her fingers in his hair, suddenly wanting to be in his arms and have all the constraints out of her way. She wanted Aaron with a need that overwhelmed her. The kiss deepened, became more passionate. She wanted to be in his arms, in his bed, making love. Would it give them a chance to fall in love?

She moaned softly, losing herself in their kiss, running one hand over his muscled shoulder, holding him with her other arm.

She realized how intense this had become and finally leaned away a fraction. Her breathing was ragged. His light brown eyes had darkened with his passion. Desire was blatant in their depths, a hungry look that fanned the fires of her own longing.

"You did well today. You're taking back another check to help people," he said, his gaze drifting over her face. "When we get back we'll go to dinner and celebrate."

"I'm glad you went with me."

He moved away and she watched as he sent a text. He lowered his phone. "I want to wait a minute in case they answer right away."

His phone beeped and he scanned the message. "You're set for Wednesday," he said, putting away his phone. "We'll go home now."

She had a tingling excitement. Part of it was relief that the talk was over and she had been able to raise some money for Royal. Part of it was wanting Aaron and knowing they would be together longer.

They met again for dinner in the dining room at the inn. Both had changed to sweaters and slacks. Throughout dinner Stella still felt bubbly excitement and when Aaron finally escorted her back to her suite, she paused at her door to put her arms around him and kiss him.

For one startled moment he stood still, but then his arm circled her waist and he kissed her in return. Without breaking the kiss, he took her key card from her, unlocked her door and stepped inside. He picked her up and let the door swing shut while she reached out to hit the light switch.

Relishing being in his arms, she let go of all the problems for a few minutes while they kissed. Their kisses were becoming more passionate, demanding. He set her on her feet and then his hands were in her hair. The long locks tumbled down as the pins dropped away. As he kissed her, his hand slipped beneath her sweater to cup her breast and then lightly caress her.

She moaned, clinging to him, on fire with wanting him. He stepped back, pulling her blue sweater over her head and tossing it aside. He unfastened her bra and cupped her full breasts lightly in his hands. "You're soft," he whispered, leaning down to kiss her and stroke her with his tongue.

She gasped with pleasure, clinging to him, wanting him with her whole being but finally stopping him and picking up her sweater to slip it over her head again.

"Aaron, I need to sort things out before we get more deeply involved, and if we make love, I'll be more involved emotionally."

"I think we're in about as deep as it gets without marriage or a permanent commitment," he said solemnly. His voice was hoarse with passion. "You can 'sort' things out. I want you, Stella. I want you in my arms, in my bed. I want to make love all night."

Every word he said made her want to walk back into his arms, but she stood still, trying to take her time the way she should have when she first met him, before she made a physical commitment. Could they fall in love if she just let go and agreed to marry him? Or would she be the only one to fall in love while Aaron still stayed coolly removed from emotional involvement or commitment?

"Aaron, we really don't know a lot about each other," she said, and that shuttered look came over his expression. A muscle worked in his jaw as he stared at her in silence.

"What would you like to know?" he asked stiffly.

"I don't know enough to ask. I just think we should get to really know each other."

He nodded. "All right, Stella. Whatever you want. Let's eat breakfast together. The more we're together, the better we'll know each other."

"I'll see you at breakfast. Thanks again for today. It was nice to raise the money for people here and to have your moral support in Lubbock today."

"Good. See you at seven in the morning."

"Sure," she said, following him to the door. He turned to look at her and she gazed into his eyes, her heart beginning to drum again as her gaze lowered to his mouth. She wanted his kisses, wanted to stop being cautious, but that's how she had gotten pregnant. Now if she let go, she might fall in love when he wouldn't. Yet, was she going to lose a chance on winning his love because of her caution? She couldn't see any future for them the way things were.

Five

The next morning after breakfast with Stella, Aaron sent text messages to three more Texas Cattleman's Club members in Dallas. Stella had given him permission to plan two meetings, so he wanted to get them arranged as soon as possible.

Next, he drove to the temporary office R&N Builders had set up in Royal. It was a flimsy, hastily built building on a back street. He saw Cole's truck already there and was surprised his partner had returned a little earlier than he had planned.

Seated at one of the small tables that served as a desk, Cole was in his usual boots, jeans and R&N

Builders T-shirt. His broad-brimmed black Resistol hung on the hat rack along with his jacket.

"How's Henry?" Aaron asked in greeting.

"He's getting along, but he needs help and he still has a lot of repairs to make. He had appointments with insurance people and an attorney about his brother's estate, so I came back here."

"I'm sorry to hear he still has a lot to do. That's tough. In the best of times there's no end to the work on a ranch."

"You got that right. And he's having a tough time about losing his brother. I figure I'm a good one to stay and give him a hand."

"I'm sure he'll appreciate it. I think a lot of people are glad to have you back in Royal. You didn't go home much before the storm."

"I've avoided being here with Craig and Paige since their marriage. I've gone home occasionally for holidays, but never was real comfortable about it since Craig and I both dated Paige in high school," Cole said, gazing into space. Aaron wondered if Cole still had feelings for Paige or if he had been in love with her when she'd married Craig.

"When the folks died, I came even less often."

He turned to look at Aaron. "I'm ready to leave for the TCC. Want to ride with me?"

"I'll drive one of the trucks because I'm going to see Stella for lunch. She raised $12,000 from people in Lubbock yesterday afternoon."

"That's good news. Royal needs whatever we can get. There's still so much to be done."

"Cole, she has an idea—she's worried about Christmas and the people who lost everything, the people with little kids who are having a hard time. She wants to have a Christmas drive to get presents."

"She's right. Those people need help. Christmas is going to be tough."

"She's getting some women together to organize it. Meanwhile TCC has its Christmas festival coming up. Sure, you and I are members of the Dallas TCC, so I don't want to come in and start asking for favors, but I'm going to this time. I thought about talking to Gil and Nathan and a few other members. It might be nice to tie this Christmas present drive to the festival and invite all those people and let them pick up their presents then. What do you think?"

"I think that's a great idea. I'd say do it."

"Also, I think we should ask the Dallas TCC to make a Christmas contribution to Royal. We could invite Dallas members to the Royal TCC Christmas Festival."

"Another good idea. We know some guys who would be willing to help and are usually generous when it's a good cause. I hope the whole town is invited this year. Everyone needs a party."

"I agree. We can talk to Gil."

"I'd be glad to," Cole replied, standing to get his jacket and hat. "I'll see you at the Cattleman's Club."

Aaron waved as he put his phone to his ear to make a call. When he was done, he stuffed some notes into his jacket pocket and locked up to go to the TCC.

When he arrived at the club, he glanced at the damage to the rambling stone and dark wood structure. Part of the slate roof of the main building had been torn off, but that had already been replaced. Trees had fallen on outbuildings, and many windows had to be replaced. A lot of the water damage had been taken care of early while the outbuildings were still in need of repair.

Aaron knew that repairs had started right away.

The sound of hammers and chainsaws had become a fixture in Royal as much as the sight of wrecking trucks hauling away debris. As Aaron parked the R&N truck and climbed out, he saw Cole talking to Nathan Battle. Cole motioned to Aaron to join them.

The tall, brown-haired sheriff shook hands with Aaron. "Glad you're here. Work keeps progressing. We have the windows replaced now and that's a relief. You get tired of looking through plastic and hearing it flap in the wind."

"I told Nathan about Stella's idea for the Christmas drive and how it might be nice to combine it with the TCC Christmas festival," Cole said.

"I think it would be great. It'll add to the festivities. The holidays can be hard enough, as both of you know too well," Nathan said. "This will be a nice way to cheer people up."

"When will Gil be here?" Aaron asked.

"He's inside now," Nathan replied. "Let's go find him. We need the president's approval before you take it to a meeting."

Aaron worked through the morning, sitting in one of the empty meeting rooms. He did take time to make some calls to set up more appointments for Stella. He grinned to himself. She might not like all the appointments he planned to get for her, but he was certain she would rise to the occasion and he would help her.

Hopefully, the makeover might help her self-confidence a little. He would talk to her about dealing with the press and interviews and then see what kind of meetings he could help her get with people who would be willing to contribute to rebuilding Royal.

He had heard people mention her for the role of acting mayor if Mayor Vance didn't recover and someone was needed to step in. He wondered whether she had heard those remarks. He suspected if she had, Stella would dismiss them as ridiculous. She had been too busy to take time to realize that she was already fulfilling the position of acting mayor.

He had to admire her in so many ways. And in private—she was about to become a lot more important to him.

He leaned back in his chair, stretching his legs. Stella was going to have his baby. The thought still shocked him. He wanted this baby to be part of his life. He had lost one child. He didn't want to lose this one. And Stella was the mother of his child. He needed to forget shock and do something nice for her right now. Neither of them were in love, but they liked being together. As he thought about it, he was startled to realize she was the first woman he had truly enjoyed being with since his wife.

That was good enough to build a relationship as far as he was concerned, and Stella was a solid, super person who was appealing and intelligent. She deserved better from him. He glanced at his watch, told Cole he was going to run an errand and left the club to head to the shops in town. He intended to do something for Stella soon. Even if he couldn't give her love, he could help her and be there for her.

Stella decided to start with Paige. They agreed to meet briefly in the small café in the Cozy Inn midmorning over coffee. Stella arrived first and waved when she saw Paige step into the wide doorway. Dressed in jeans, a navy sweater, Western boots and a denim jacket, she crossed the room and sat at the small table across from Stella.

"What's up?"

"Thanks for taking time out of your busy day. I want to ask you a favor. I'm concerned about how hard Christmas will be on the people who lost so much in the storm," she said. "Christmas—any holiday—is a tough time when you've lost loved ones, your home, everything. I know you suffered a devastating loss, so if it upsets you to deal with this, Paige, say so and bow out. I'll understand."

"No. The holiday is going to be hard for a lot of people."

"Well, there are some people here who can't afford to have any kind of Christmas after all they lost. It's another hurt on top of a hurt. This is about the people who can't afford to get presents for their kids, for their families, who'll be alone and don't have much, that sort of thing."

"They should have help. What did you have in mind?"

"A Christmas drive with gifts and maybe monetary donations for them so they can buy things."

"Stella, I think that's grand. Thank goodness we can afford to do things at Christmas. But you're right about some of these people who have been hurt in every sort of way including financially. I think a Christmas drive to get presents would be wonderful. I'm so glad you thought about that."

"Well, what I really want— I need a cochair and you would be perfect if you'd do it. I know you're busy—"

Shaking her auburn hair away from her face, Paige smiled. "Stop there. I think it's a good cause so, yes, I'll cochair this project."

"That's so awesome," Stella said, smiling at her friend. "I can always count on you. I'm going to call some others to be on our committee."

"If you need my help, I can ask some friends for you."

"Here's my list. I've already sent a text to Lark and I left a message. I'll call Megan and my friend Edie."

"I can talk to Beth and Julie. I know Amanda Battle and I think she would help."

"I have my lists. We'll have a Christmas tree in the temporary town hall or I can get some of the merchants to take tags and hang them in their windows. We can make little paper ornaments and hang them on merchant's Christmas trees. Each ornament will match up with a person who will receive a gift. The recipients can choose an ornament and take it home. They'll match up with our master list, so we can tell who gets what present and we won't have to use names. So, for instance, the ornament could read, 'Boy—eight years old' plus a number to match our list and suggested gift ideas. We'll need to have gifts for the adults, too."

"Sounds good to me. We'll need to set up a Christmas-drive fund at one of the banks, so people can get tax credit for their donations," Paige said.

"I can deal with that because I'll be going by the bank anyway," Stella said.

"Fine. You take care of setting up the bank account."

"Paige, I appreciate this so much. I talked to Aaron about it and he'll run it past Cole and the TCC guys. I have a list of people who will probably participate in the drive. I'll email it to you."

"Good. I better run."

"Thanks again. I'll walk out with you. I'm going to the office—our temporary one. I think town hall will be one of the last places to get back to normal."

"There are so many places that still need to get fixed, including the Double R," she said.

"How're you doing running that ranch by your-self?"

"I run it in Craig's place, but not by myself. Our hands have been wonderful. They've really pitched in and gone the extra mile."

"I'm glad. See you soon."

They parted and Stella drove to town hall, try-ing to focus on work there and stop thinking about Aaron.

It was seven when she went down to meet Aaron in the Cozy Inn dining room, which had gotten to be a daily occurrence. She thought about how much she looked forward to being with him as she glanced once more at her reflection in the mirror in the elevator. Her hair was in a neat bun, every hair in place. She wore a thick pale yellow sweater and dark brown slacks with her practical shoes. The night air was chilly, although it was warm in the inn.

She stepped off the elevator and saw him only a few yards away.

Tonight he was in slacks, a thick navy sweater and Western boots. He looked sexy and appeal-ing and she hoped he asked her to dance.

"You're not in your usual spot tonight. I thought maybe you decided not to come," she said.

"Never. And if something ever does interfere with my meeting you when I said I would, believe me I'll call and let you know unless I've been knocked unconscious."

She laughed. "I hope not. I had a productive day, did you?"

"Oh, yes, I did. Let's get a table and I'll tell you all about it, because a lot of it concerns you. I'll bet they were pleased at town hall with the checks you got yesterday."

"Oh, my, yes. We have three families that are in a desperate situation and need money for a place to stay. Then some of it will go to buy more supplies where needed. Do you want me to keep going down the list?"

"No need." He paused to talk to the maître d', who led them to a table near the fireplace. Mesquite logs had been tossed in with the other logs and the pungent smell was inviting.

Stella ordered ice water again. When they were alone, she smiled at him. "I saw Paige Richardson today. She agreed to cochair my Christmas-drive committee."

"You didn't waste time getting that going."

"No, we need to as soon as possible. Actually, I kept $2,000 of the check from Lubbock to open a fund at the bank for the Christmas drive. She is recruiting some more members for the committee and I have Megan's and Julie's help."

"I talked to Cole about it and then we talked to Gil Addison and Nathan Battle and the TCC is willing to tie the Christmas drive in with their Christmas festival. They'll invite all the families and children to receive their gifts during the festival."

"That's wonderful, Aaron. Thank you. Paige was going to contact Amanda Battle and see if she will be on our committee."

"That's a good person to contact. So you're off to a roaring start there."

"Now tell me more about the Dallas trip."

"Here comes our waiter and then we'll talk."

They ordered and she waited expectantly. "Next week you have one little fifteen-minute spot on the noon news in Fort Worth. This will be your chance to kick off the Christmas drive and maybe get some donations for it."

"I'm looking forward to getting news out about the Christmas drive."

"Good. That night I have the oil and gas executives lined up. We will meet them for dinner and you can talk to them about the storm and what people need. I know you'll reach them emotionally because you have so many touching stories."

"Thank you. I'll be happy to do all of these things but I still say I wasn't meant to be a fundraiser," she said, suspecting she wasn't changing his mind at all.

"You'll be great. You'll be fine. You've been doing this sort of thing since the storm. I've seen your interviews. I even taped one. You're a natural."

"Aaron, every cell in your body is filled with self-assurance. You can't possibly understand having butterflies or qualms."

"I have to admit, I'm not burdened with being afraid to talk to others about subjects I know."

Smiling, she shook her head. "I don't know everything about my subject."

"You know as much as anybody else in Royal and more about the storm than about ninety-eight percent of the population. You went through it, for heaven's sake. You were at town hall. You were there for all the nightmarish first hours after the storm and you've been there constantly ever since. I heard you crawled under debris and rescued someone. Is that right?"

"Yes. I could hear the cries. She was under a big slab of concrete that was held up by rubble. Not fun, but we got her out. It was a twenty-year-old woman."

"That's impressive," he said, studying her as if he hadn't ever seen her before. "If you did that, you can talk to people in an interview. After we eat let's go up to your room or mine and go over ways you can handle the interview."

When their tossed green salads came, Aaron continued to talk. She realized he was giving her good advice on things to do and she soaked up every word, feeling she would do better the next appearance she made.

Aaron kept up his advice and encouragement throughout the meal, and when they were through dinner, Stella didn't want him to stop. "Aaron, why don't we go to my room now and you can continue coaching me?"

"Sure, but a couple of dances first," he said,

standing and taking her hand. In minutes she was in his arms, moving with him on the dance floor, relishing dancing, being in his arms.

Aaron was becoming important to her. She was falling in love with him, but would he ever let go and fall in love with her? She felt he always held himself back and she still had that feeling with him. There couldn't be any real love between them until all barriers were gone.

Was she making a mistake by rejecting intimacy when Aaron obviously wanted it, as well as wanted to marry her? The question still constantly plagued her.

In the slow dances, their steps were in perfect unison as if they had danced together for years. Sometimes she felt she had known him well and for a long time. Other times she realized what strangers they were to each other. Sometimes when he got that shuttered look and she could feel him withdrawing, she was certain she should tell him goodbye and get him out of her life now. Yet with a baby between them, breaking off from seeing Aaron was impossible.

When the music ended they left and went to her suite. He got the tape of her interview.

"Want something to drink while we watch?" she asked. "Hot chocolate? Beer?"

"Hot chocolate sounds good. Go easy on the chocolate. I'll help."

They sat on the sofa and he put on the tape. While they watched, Aaron gave her pointers and when the tape ended, he talked about dealing with the press. Removing pins from her hair, he talked about doing interviews. As the first locks fell, she looked up at him.

"You don't need to keep your hair up all the time. You surely don't sleep all night this way."

"Of course not. It wouldn't stay thirty minutes."

"So, we'll just take it down a little early to-night," he said. "Now back to the press. Get their cards and get their names, learn their names when you meet them. They have all sorts of contacts and can open doors for you."

As she listened to him talk, she paid attention, but she was also aware of her hair falling over her back and shoulders, of Aaron's warm breath on her nape and his fingers brushing lightly against her. Every touch added a flame to the fires burning inside. Desire was hot, growing more intense the longer she sat with him. She wanted his kiss.

She should learn what he was telling her, but Aaron's kisses seemed more important. When the bun was completely undone, he placed the pins on a nearby table. He parted her hair, placing thick strands of it over each shoulder as he leaned closer to brush light kisses across her nape.

Catching her breath, she inhaled deeply. Desire built, a hungry need to turn and wrap her arms around him, to kiss him.

She felt his tongue on her nape, his kisses trailing on her skin. He picked her up, lifting her to his lap. She gazed into his brown eyes while her heart raced and she could barely get her breath.

"I want you, Aaron. You make me want you," she whispered. She leaned closer to kiss him, her tongue going deep. Her heartbeat raced as she wrapped her arms around his neck.

His hands slipped lightly beneath her sweater, sliding up to cup her breasts. In minutes he cupped each breast in his hands, caressing her. She moaned with pleasure and need, wanting more of him. She wanted to be alone with him. To make love and shut out the world and the future and just know tonight.

Would that bring him closer to her? Her to him?

She couldn't marry him without love, but intimacy might be a way to love.

She tightened her arms, pressing against his solid warmth, holding him as they kissed. His fingers moved over her, touching lightly, caressing her, unfastening snaps, unfastening her bra.

His fingers trailed down over her ribs, down to her slacks. While they kissed, she felt his fingers twisting free buttons. Without breaking their kiss, he picked her up and carried her into her bedroom. Light spilled through the doorway from the front room, providing enough illumination to see. He stood her on her feet by the bed and continued to kiss her, leaning over her, holding her against him as his hand slipped down to take off her slacks.

She stepped out of them and kicked off her shoes, looking up at him for a moment as she gasped for breath.

Combing his fingers into her hair on either side of her face, he looked down at her. "I want you. I want to make love to you all night long."

"Aaron—"

He kissed her again, stopping any protest she might have made, but she wasn't protesting. She wanted him, this strong man who had been at her side for so much now, who was willing to do the honorable thing and marry her. She wanted his love. She wanted him with her, loving her. That might not ever happen if she kept pushing him away.

He tugged her sweater up, pulling it over her head and tossing it aside. Her unfastened bra slipped down and she let it fall to the floor. Cupping her breasts again, he trailed light kisses over her while she clung to him and gasped with pleasure. When he tossed away his sweater, she ran her hands across his chest, stroking his hard muscles, caressing him lightly.

Wanting to steal his heart, she kissed him.

It was an impossible, unreasonable fantasy. Yet she could love him until he found it difficult to resist her and impossible to walk away. Would she ensnare her own heart in trying to win his?

He placed his hands on her waist, stepping back to look at her, his gaze a burning brand. "You're beautiful, so soft," he whispered, and leaned forward to trail kisses over her breasts.

Desire continued to build, to be a fire she couldn't control. She wanted him now and there were no arguments about whether she should or shouldn't make love with him. She unfastened his slacks, letting them fall, and then removed his briefs. He pulled her close, their bare bodies pressed together, and even that wasn't enough. Again, he picked her up and turned to place her on the bed, kneeling and then stretching beside her to kiss her while his hands roamed over her to caress her.

She moaned softly, a sound taken by his kisses. Now union seemed necessary, urgent. Her hands drifted over him, down his smooth back, over his hard butt and along a muscled thigh.

He moved, kneeling beside her, looking at her as his hands played over her and then he trailed kisses over her knees, up the inside of her thighs, parting her legs, kissing and stroking her.

Arching beneath his touch, she wanted more of him. Her eyes were shut as he toyed with her, building need. One of his hands was between her thighs, the other tracing her breasts, light touches that drove her wild until she rose to her knees to kiss and stroke him.

His eyes were stormy, dark with desire. Need shook her because of his intensity. His groan was deep in his throat while his fingers locked in her hair and she held and kissed him, her tongue stroking him slowly. He gasped and slipped his hands beneath her arm to raise her.

He kissed her hard, one arm circling her waist, holding her close against him, his other hand running over her, caressing her and building need to a fever pitch.

She clung to him as she kissed him. "Aaron," she whispered. "Let's make love—"

They fell on the bed and he moved over her as she spread her legs for him and arched to meet him, wanting him physically as much as she wanted his love.

He entered her slowly, filling her, taking his time while he lowered himself, moving close to kiss her.

When he partially withdrew, she raised her hips, clinging to him to draw him back.

"Aaron, I want you," she whispered.

He slowly entered her again, and she gasped with pleasure, thrashing beneath him and running her hands over his back. He loved her with slow deliberation, maintaining control, trying to increase her pleasure as she moved beneath him and her need and desire built. Her pulse roared in her ears as his mouth covered hers again in another hungry kiss that increased her need.

Caught in a compelling desire that drove her beyond thought to just react to every stroke and touch and kiss from him, she tugged him closer, moving faster beneath him.

Beaded in sweat, he rocked with her until she reached a pinnacle and burst over it, rapture pouring over her while she moved wildly. When his control ended, he thrust deeply and fast.

Arching against him, she shuddered with another climax. Letting go, she slowed as ecstasy enveloped her.

"Aaron, love," she cried, without realizing what she had said.

Aaron groaned and finally slowed, his weight coming down partially on her. He turned his head to kiss her lightly.

While each gasped for breath, they lay wrapped in each other's arms. Gradually, their breathing slowed until it was deep and regular. He rolled to his side, keeping her with him.

She opened her eyes to look at him and he kissed her lightly again.

"I don't want to let go of you," he whispered.

"I don't want you to," she answered, trailing her fingers over his chest, feeling rock-solid muscles. She kept her mind closed to everything except the present moment and enjoying being in his arms and having made love with him.

"Stella, if you would marry me, we could have this all the time," he whispered, toying with a lock of her long hair.

She didn't feel like talking and she didn't care to argue, so she kept quiet, still stroking him.

They held each other in a silence that was comfortable for her. She suspected it was for him, too. She knew he wasn't asleep because he continued to play with strands of her hair. He had to know she was awake, because she still ran her fingers lightly over him, touching, caressing, loving him.

"Before I commit to marriage, I will have to be deeply in love and so will you. If that happens, we'll both know it and the rest of the world will know it. We're not at that point. We're not in love with each other," she said, the words sounding bleak to her.

"I still say it could come in marriage."

"I don't want to take that chance," she whispered, hoping she wasn't throwing away her future and her baby's future in a few glib sentences that were easy to say when she was being held close to his heart.

"Think about it. We're good together, Stella."

She raised herself slightly on her elbow, propping her head on her hand, and looked down at him. "You think about it. Do you want a marriage without love?"

Again, she got that look from him as if he had closed a door between them. She felt as if he had just gone away from her, almost as if he had left the room even though he was still right here beside her. An ache came to her heart. Aaron had closed himself off. There was a part of his life he wouldn't share, and with time it could become a wedge between them.

She thought about asking him what made him withdraw into a shell, but she suspected that would only make him do so more and make things worse.

"No, I suppose you're right. I don't want that," he answered, and she heard a note of steel in his voice.

"Maybe things will change if we keep seeing each other."

"I want to be in my child's life, so someday we'll have to work out how we're going to share our baby," he said in a different tone of voice. Why had he changed? Only minutes ago he hadn't been this way. She wondered whether they would ever be truly close, much less truly in love.

She lay down beside him again, her hair spreading on his shoulder as he pulled her close against him, leg against leg, thigh against thigh, her head on the indention between his chest and shoulder. He had proposed. He'd helped her. He wanted to be with her and take her out. What had happened in his life to cause him to let it get between him and someone else he would otherwise be close to in a relationship?

Would he ever feel close enough to her to share whatever he held back from her now?

Six

"Hey, why so solemn?" he asked, nuzzling her neck and making her giggle.

"That's better. Let's go shower and see what happens."

"Evidently you have plans," she said, amused and forgetting the serious life-changing decisions that loomed for her.

He stepped out of bed, scooped her up and carried her to the large bathroom, to stand her on her feet in the roomy tiled shower.

They played and splashed beneath the warm water until he looked at her and his smile faded, desire surfacing in his eyes. He reached out to caress her breasts and she inhaled, placing her hands on his hips and closing her eyes.

He was aroused, ready to love again, and she wanted him. She stroked him, stepping closer to kiss him and hold him. His lips were wet, his face wet, his body warm and wet against hers.

He turned off the water and moved from the shower, taking her hand as she stepped out. Aaron picked up a thick towel, shaking it out and lightly drying her in sensuous strokes that heightened desire. She picked up another fresh towel to dry him, excited by the look in his eyes that clearly revealed desire.

She rubbed the thick white towel over sculpted muscles, down over his flat belly, lightly drawing it across his thick staff.

He groaned, dropping his towel and grabbing hers to toss it away. He scooped her into his arms and carried her back to bed as he kissed her. Their legs were still wet, but she barely noticed and didn't care as she clung to him and kissed him.

He shifted between her legs and then rose up slightly, watching her as he entered her again. She cried out, arching to meet him, reaching for him to pull him back down into her embrace.

They made love frantically as if they never had before and she cried out with her climax.

He climaxed soon after, holding her as he pumped, finally lowering his weight and then rolling on his side to hold her against him.

"Fantastic, Aaron," she whispered, floating in euphoria. "Hot kisses and sexy loving."

"I'll have to agree," he said. "I want to hold you all night."

"No arguments from me on that one."

Once again they were silent and she ran her hand over him, thinking she would never tire of touching him. Aaron brought joy, help, fun, excitement, sex into her life. He was giving her his baby. If only he could give her his love.

"This has cut short all your help with giving interviews and dealing with the press."

"I'm still here and we'll continue. Besides, you're a fast learner."

"You don't really know that, but I'm trying. Aaron, when we fly to Dallas on Tuesday, I want to visit with my mom in Fort Worth. I called her and we made plans to have lunch. She's meeting me on her lunch hour and my grandmother has gone to Abilene to stay a week with my aunt.

You're welcome to join us for lunch if you want, but you don't have to do that."

"I'll pass because you don't see her real often, so she may want to talk to you alone. I've got a limo for you—"

"A limo? Aaron, that's ridiculous. I can rent a car at the airport."

"No need. Cole and I have a limo service we use and two men who regularly drive for us. Sid will drive you Tuesday. He'll take you to Fort Worth for lunch and the interview and then he'll drive you back to a shop I recommend in Dallas where you can buy some new dresses. He'll either wait or give you a number and you can call him when you're ready to be picked up."

"I'm beginning to feel like your mistress."

Aaron laughed. "This is for Royal. I expect you to get a lot of donations for the town. Just keep thinking about the good we can do. Now if you would like to be my mistress—"

"Forget that one," she said, and he chuckled.

"We'll get back to talking about business to-morrow. Tonight I have other things on my mind. You don't have any morning sickness, do you?"

"Not a bit so far. I just can't eat as much and

sometimes I get sleepy about two in the afternoon."

"Why don't you catch a few winks. The world
won't stop spinning if you do. You're vital to
Royal, Stella. You've done a superb job, but the
world will go on without you for the time it takes
you to get a good night's sleep."

"Thank you, Dr. Nichols. How much do I owe
you for that advice?"

"About two dozen kisses," he said, and she
laughed, pushing him on his back and rolling over
on top of him.

"I'm going to pay you now."

"Best collection I'll ever make," he said, wrapping his arms around her.

Aaron stirred and rolled over to look at Stella.
She lay on her back, one arm flung out, her hair
spread over the pillow. She was covered to her
chin by the sheet. Even in her sleep she stayed all
covered, which amused him.

She continued to fill in for the mayor. It amazed
him how people turned to her for help, everyone
from the city treasurer to ordinary citizens. He
didn't think Stella was even aware of the scope of

what she was doing for the citizens of Royal. She was one of the key people in restoring the town and securing assistance for people. She was willing to accept his help and he could introduce her to so many people who would contribute to rebuilding Royal. He liked being with her. He liked making love with her. She excited him, and the more he got to know her, the more he enjoyed her. If she would agree to marriage, he thought, with time they would come to really love each other.

He thought of Paula and Blake, and the dull pain came as it always did.

Along with it came second thoughts. Maybe he was wrong about never being able to love someone else again. And maybe Stella was right—the only time to marry someone would be if he was as wildly in love as he had been with Paula. If he only married to give his baby a father, and wasn't really in love, that wouldn't be fair to Stella and might not ever be a happy arrangement.

He thought the fact that they got along well now and he liked being with her would be enough. The sex was fantastic. But there was more to life than that.

He sighed. He wanted to know this baby of his.

He wanted to be a dad for his child, to watch him or her grow up. Aaron wanted to be a part of that.

If he didn't marry her, she could marry someone else who would take her far away where Aaron wouldn't get to see his son or daughter often. Maybe he needed to contact one of his lawyers and get some advice. The one thing he was certain about—he did not want to lose his second child.

He lifted a strand of Stella's hair. She excited him and he liked being with her. She was level-headed, practical. If he gave it a little more time and attention, maybe they could fall in love.

He had been a widower for seven years now. How likely was he to change?

If anyone could work a change, it would be Stella. She had already done some miracles in Royal. If Mayor Vance recovered, someone should tell him exactly how much Stella had stepped in and taken over.

Desire stirred. There might not be love, but there was a growing fiery attraction for both of them. He wanted to be with her and he was going to miss her when he returned to Dallas. Right now that wasn't going to happen—without her being beside him—until after the holidays. He would worry about that when it came time for them to part.

He leaned down to brush a kiss on her temple as he pushed the sheet lower to bare her breasts so he could caress her. Then he shifted to reach her so he could trail light kisses over her full breasts. Beneath those buttoned-up blouses she wore, there were some luscious curves.

She stirred, opened her eyes and blinked. Then she smiled and wrapped her arms around his neck, pulling him down so she could kiss him.

Forgetting his worries, Aaron wrapped his arms around her, drawing her close as he kissed her passionately.

It was Saturday, but still like a workday for her with all that needed to be done in Royal. She glanced at the clock and sat up, yanking the sheet beneath her arms. Alarmed, she glanced at Aaron. "Aaron, it's nine in the morning," she said, horrified how late they had slept. "Aaron."

He opened his eyes and reached up to pull her down. She wriggled away. "Oh, no, you don't. We've got to get out of this bed."

Looking amused, he drew her to him. "No, we

don't. It's Saturday. Come here and let me show you the best possible way to start our weekend."

"Aaron, I work on Saturday. Royal needs all sorts of things. I have a list of things to do."

"Any appointments with people?"

"I don't think so, just things to do."

"Like finding Dobbin and locking up Mr. Sherman's house?"

"Maybe so, but I spend Saturdays doing those things. I don't lollygag in bed."

"Let me show you my way of lollygagging in bed." He pulled her closer.

"Aaron, look—"

He kissed away her words, his hand lightly fondling her, caressing her breast while he kissed her thoroughly. He raised up to roll over so he was above her as he kissed her.

She was stiff in his arms for about ten seconds and then she melted against him, knowing she was lost.

It was two hours later when she grabbed the sheet and stepped out of bed. "Aaron, I'm going to shower alone," she said emphatically. "There are things I think I should do today and if someone came looking for either one of us, I would be mortified."

He grinned. "You shouldn't be. First, it's none of anyone else's business. Second—and most important—you're passing up a chance to spend a day in bed with me."

She had to laugh. "You do tempt me beyond belief, but I know there are things I can get done and sooner or later someone will ask me to help in some manner. I'm going to shower."

She heard him chuckle as she left the room. When she came out of the shower, he was nowhere around. As she looked through the suite, she realized he must have left.

She found a note and picked it up. In scrawling writing, she read, "Meet me in the dining room in twenty minutes."

"Twenty minutes from when?" she said aloud to no one. She shook her head and went to get dressed to go to the dining room and eat with him.

She spent the day running the errands on her list, making calls, going by the hospital again. At dinner she ate with Aaron, and for a short time after he talked to her more about dealing with the press, until she was in his lap, his kisses ending the coaching session on how to deal with the press.

They had grown more intimate, spent more time together, yet he still shut himself and his past off from her.

She could ask someone else about Aaron, but she wanted him to get close enough to her to stop keeping part of himself shut away. Moments still came when she could sense him emotionally withdrawing and at those times, she thought they would never really be close or deeply in love with each other. Not in love enough to marry.

Why was true intimacy so difficult for Aaron when he was so open about other aspects of his life?

The days leading up to the Dallas trip flew by.

Sunday morning Aaron went to church with her. After the service he stood to one side waiting as people greeted her and stopped to talk briefly.

When she finally joined him to go eat Sunday dinner, he smiled at her.

"What are you smiling about?"

"You. How can you lack one degree of confidence about talking to crowds? You had as long a line of people waiting to speak to you as the preacher did."

She laughed. "You're exaggerating. They were just saying good morning."

"Uh-huh. It looked like an earnest conversation three or four times."

"Maybe one or two had problems."

"Sure, Stella. Sometime today or tomorrow I'll bet you do something about those problems."

"Okay, you win. I still say helping people one-on-one is different from talking to a group of people I don't know and trying to get them to donate to the relief effort in Royal."

He grinned and squeezed her arm lightly. "Let's go eat. We missed breakfast."

By midafternoon she was in bed again with Aaron. She felt giddy, happy, and knew she was in love with him. She might have huge regrets later, but right now, she was having the time of her life with him.

Sunday night while she was in his arms in bed, she turned to look at him. "You should either go home now or plan to get up very early because Monday will be a busy day."

"I'll opt for the get-up-early choice," he drawled,

toying with locks of her hair. "The more time with you, the better life is."

"I hope you mean that," she said, suddenly serious.

He shifted to hold her closer. "I mean it or I wouldn't have said it." He kissed her and their conversation ended.

Monday, after breakfast with Aaron, she got back on track with appointments and meetings. Later that afternoon, she had another brief meeting with Paige at the Cozy Inn café.

"Paige, we need to have a meeting with everyone who wants to be on this committee. I've talked to Megan Maguire, Gloria Holt, Keaton's mom, Lark Taylor, Edith Simms—they all volunteered to help us. I told Lark that Keaton's mom had volunteered and Lark said she still wanted to be a volunteer. I think it will all be harmonious."

"Great. I have Beth, Amanda Battle and Julie Kingston. This is such a good idea, Stella. It would have been dreadful if we'd ignored these people at this time of year."

"Someone would have thought of it if we hadn't. But it's especially nice to do this in conjunction with the TCC Christmas festival. Also, I intend to raise some money beyond what we'll need for getting presents. It'll be wonderful to have people bring presents for those who lost so much, but I also want them to get cash to spend as they want to. Everyone wants to give their children something they've selected. Donated presents are wonderful, but giving these families a chance to buy and wrap their own gifts is important, too."

"Another good idea, Stella. You're filled with them."

"'Tis the season. I'll be in Dallas tomorrow and gone for the rest of the week. Aaron has made appointments for me to meet people he thinks will be willing and able to help Royal."

"That's good. I'll take care of the Christmas drive while you're gone. You see if you can get some more donations."

"Thanks for all your help," Stella said, giving Paige's hand a squeeze, always sorry for Paige's losses.

After they parted, Stella went to the hospital. Mayor Vance was improving and now he could have visitors. She knocked lightly on the door and his wife called to come in.

The mayor was propped up in bed. His legs

were in casts and he was connected to machines with tubes on both sides of the bed.

"He's sitting up now and he's on the mend," his wife said.

"Mayor Vance, I am so happy to see you," Stella said, walking closer. He had always been thin, but now he was far thinner and pale, his dark brown hair a bigger contrast with his pale complexion. His brown eyes were lively and she was glad he was improving.

"Stella, it's good of you to come by. I've heard you've been a regular and I've heard so many good things about you. I could always count on you at the office."

"Thank you. The whole town has pulled together. Support for Royal has poured in—it amazes me and the donations to the Royal storm recovery fund grow steadily."

"That's so good to hear. It doesn't seem possible the tornado happened more than two months ago. It's almost mid-December and here I am still in the hospital."

"At least you're getting better," she said, smiling at him and his wife.

"I've talked with members of the town council. We need an acting mayor and I hope you'll be willing to do it."

"Mayor Vance, thank you for the vote of confidence, but I think there are more qualified people. I'm sure the town council has others in mind."

"I've heard all the things you've been doing and what you did the first twenty-four hours after the storm hit. You're the one, Stella. I'm pushing for you so don't let me down. From the sound of it, you're already doing the job."

"Well, I'll think about it," she said politely, wanting to avoid arguing with him in her first visit with him since the storm. "We've had so much help from other places that it's really wonderful."

She sat and visited a few more minutes and then left. His wife followed her into the hall.

"Stella, thanks again for coming. You've been good to check on him through all this."

"I'm glad to see he's getting better steadily."

"We're grateful. Come again. Think about what he said about filling in for him. He can't go back for a long time."

"I will," Stella said, maintaining a pleasant expression as she left and promptly dismissing the conversation.

* * *

Tuesday morning she flew to Dallas with Aaron. He picked up his car at an agency near the airport and they headed to his house in a gated suburb north of the city.

"We'll leave our things at my house. I've got the limo for you, and Sid will drive you to Fort Worth for lunch with your mother and next, to your interview at the Fort Worth TV station. After that he'll drive you back to Dallas to a dress shop while I go to the office. If you're having a makeover, you should have some new clothes. Get four or five dresses and a couple of suits."

"Seriously?" she asked, laughing. "Have you lost it, Aaron? I don't need one new thing, much less a bunch."

"Yes, you do for the people I'll introduce you to."

"When you tell me things like that, I get butterflies again."

"Ignore them and they'll vanish. Buy some new duds and shoes—the whole thing. This is an investment in Royal. Get something elegant, Stella."

She laughed again. "Aaron, you're talking to

me, Stella. I don't need to look elegant to climb over debris in Royal."

"You need to look elegant to raise money so we can get rid of the debris in Royal."

She studied his profile, wondering what he was getting her into and if she could do what he wanted. Would it really help Royal? She thought about the money she had raised in Lubbock and took a deep breath. She would give it a try. "You're changing me," she said, thinking about how that was true in every way possible.

He picked up her hand to brush a kiss across her knuckles while he kept his attention on the highway. "Maybe you're changing me, too," he said.

Startled, she focused more intently on him. How had she made even the tiniest change in his life?

He remained focused on his driving, but he had sounded serious when he spoke. Was she really causing any changes in his life? Continually, ordinary things popped up that reminded her how little she really knew about him, and his last remark was just another one of them.

"Aaron, you and I don't really know each other. You don't talk about yourself much," she said, wondering how many times she had told him the same thing before.

"I think you should be grateful for that one. Also, I think we're getting to know each other rather well. We can work on that when we're home alone tonight."

"I didn't mean physically."

"Whoa—that's a letdown. You got me all excited there," he teased.

"Stop. Your imagination is running away with you," she said, and he grinned.

They finally arrived at his neighborhood and went through the security gate. Tall oaks lined the curving drive and she glimpsed an occasional mansion set back on landscaped lawns through the trees.

"This isn't where I pictured you living."

"I'm not sure I want to ask what you pictured."

"Just not this big." She looked at the immaculate lawns with multicolored flowerbeds. In many ways Aaron's everyday life was far removed from her own. Even so, he was doing so much for her, including all he had set up for today.

"Aaron, thanks for doing all this for me. The appointments, the opportunities to help Royal, the salon visit. I appreciate everything."

With a quick glance, he smiled at her. "I'm happy to help because you've been doing a great job."

"The mayor seemed happy with reports he's had of what's been happening and I'm glad. It would be terrible if he felt pressured to get out of the hospital and back to work."

"I'm sure he's getting good reports. I think he'll get more good reports from what you do today."

"You're an optimist, Aaron."

"It's easy where you're concerned," he said, and she smiled at him. "Earlier, I talked to Cecelia at the dress shop and she'll help you. We're friends and I've known her a long time. Pick several things so you have a choice. It'll go on my bill. You don't even have to take my credit card. If you don't choose something, I will, and I promise you, you won't like that."

She shook her head. "Very well, I won't argue with you, because you won't give up. Don't forget, I'm meeting my mom at half past eleven. You're welcome to join us."

"Thanks, but I have a lot of catching up to do at

the office and you and your mom will enjoy being by yourselves. What I will do, if you want me to be there, is meet you at the television station for the interview."

"You don't need to drive to Fort Worth to hold my hand through an interview," she said, smiling. "I can do this one alone. Now tonight, you better join me."

"I'll be with you tonight."

"Buying more clothes and going to a salon will be a whole new experience," she said. "Aaron, I think I can raise just as much money looking the way I already look."

"Humor me. We'll see. I think you can raise more and you'll be more at ease on television for interviews."

"I don't think clothes will make a bit of difference."

He grinned. "Clothes will make all kinds of difference. You go on television without any and you'll get so much money—"

"Aaron, you know what I mean," she interrupted, and they both laughed. She had fun with him and he was helpful to her. She gazed at him and wished she didn't still feel some kind of barrier between them, because he was growing more important to her daily. And she was falling more in love with him daily while she didn't think his feelings toward her had changed at all.

They passed through another set of iron gates after Aaron entered a code. When he drove up a winding drive to a sprawling three-story house, she was shocked at the size and obvious wealth it represented. "You have a magnificent home."

"I'm in the construction business, remember?"

She rode in silence, looking at the mansion that was far too big for one person. It was just another reminder of how little she knew about Aaron and how closed off he was about himself.

When he parked at the back of the house and came around the car to open the door for her, she stepped out. Stella stood quietly staring at him and he paused.

"What?" he asked. "Something's worrying you."

"I don't even know you."

He studied her a moment and then stepped forward, his arm going around her waist as he pulled her against him and kissed her. For a startled moment she was still and then she wrapped her arms around him to return the kiss.

"I'd say you know me," he said to her when he released her.

As she stepped back, she waved her hand at the house. "This is not what I envisioned."

"You'll get accustomed to it. C'mon, let me show you your room," he said, retrieving their bags from the back.

"We'll take a tour later," he said, walking through a kitchen that was big enough to hold her entire suite at the Cozy Inn. It had dark oak walls and some of the state-of-the-art appliances had a dark wood finish.

She walked beside him down a wide hallway, turning as hallways branched off in opposite directions. He stepped into the first open doorway. "How's this?" he asked, placing her bag on a suitcase stand.

She looked around a spacious, beautiful room with Queen Anne furniture, dark and light blue decor and thick area rugs.

"I'll get my mail and you can meet me in the kitchen. As soon as you're ready, we'll go to town. It'll give you more time to shop and I need to get to the office." He stepped closer, placing his hands on her shoulders and lowering his voice.

"There are other things I'd rather do this morning, but with your appointments we better stick to business."

"I agree. You check your mail and I'll meet you."

He nodded and left.

Twenty minutes later, he stood waiting in the kitchen when she returned. "The limo's here. C'mon and I'll introduce you to Sid."

When they stepped outside, a brown-haired man who looked to be in his twenties waited by a white limo. He smiled as they walked up.

"Hi, Sid," Aaron said. "Stella, meet Sid Fryer. Sid, this is Ms. Daniels."

"Glad to meet you, Sid," she said.

"She's going to Cecelia's shop later and you can hang around or give her a number and she'll call you. She'll be there two hours minimum," Aaron instructed.

Stella was surprised. She couldn't imagine spending that much time picking out dresses.

Sid held the limo door for her and she climbed inside, turning to the window as Aaron stepped away and waved.

Sid climbed behind the wheel and they left.

When she glanced back, Aaron was already in his car.

"Sid—?"

He glanced at her in the rearview mirror. "Yes, ma'am?"

"Just call me Stella. Everyone does in my hometown of Royal. I just can't be that formal—we'll be together off and on all day."

She could see him grin in the rearview mirror. "Yes, ma'am. Whatever you say."

When Sid turned out of the gated area where Aaron lived, Stella looked behind them and saw Aaron turning the opposite way.

She met her mother in a coffee shop near the high school where her mother was principal. As Stella approached the booth where her mother sat looking at papers on the table, she realized where she got her plain way of dressing and living. Her mother's hair was in a roll, fastened on the back of her head. She wore a brown blouse and skirt, practical low-heel shoes and no makeup. Stella hadn't told her mother about the pregnancy yet and intended to today, but as she looked at her mother bent over her papers, she decided to wait a bit longer, until she had made more definite plans for raising the child. Her mother would probably want to step in and take charge, although she was deeply wrapped up in her job and, in the past few years, had interacted very little with either Stella or her sister.

Stella greeted her mother, gave her a slight hug and a light kiss on the cheek and slid into the booth across from her. "How are you?" Stella asked.

"So busy with the end of the semester coming. I can only stay an hour because I have a stack of papers on my desk I have to deal with and three appointments with parents this afternoon. How are things in Royal?"

"Slowly improving."

"I've seen you in television clips. It looks as if you're busy. When will the mayor take over again so you won't have to do his job for him?"

"Mom, he was hurt badly and was on the critical list for a long time. The deputy mayor was killed."

"I'm glad I moved out of Royal. You should give it thought."

"I'll do that," she said, reminded again of why she was so much closer to her sister than her mother.

They talked over salads and then her mother gathered up papers and said she had to get back to her office. Stella kissed her goodbye and waited a few minutes before calling Sid for the limo— something she did not want to have to explain to her mother.

Sid drove her to the television station. Everyone she dealt with welcomed her and was so friendly that she was at ease immediately. A smiling receptionist let the host know Stella had arrived and in minutes a smiling blonde appeared and extended her hand.

"Welcome. I'm Natalia Higgens and we're delighted to have you on the show."

"Thank you," Stella said, shaking the woman's hand and relaxing. "I hope this does some good for my hometown."

"We're happy to have you and sorry about Royal. The tornado was dreadful. I think our viewers will be interested and I think you'll get some support. We'll show a short video one of our reporters made after the storm. I'll have some questions for you. People are responsive when someone has been hurt and you have a town filled with people who have been hurt."

"I really appreciate this opportunity to try to get help for Royal."

"We're glad to air your story. If you'll come with me."

Fifteen minutes later, Natalia Higgens made her brief introduction, looking at the camera. "The F4 tornado struck at 4:14 p.m. on October 6th, a Monday." The camera cut to the video the studio had taken after the storm. As soon as the video ended, Natalia turned to ask Stella about Royal.

From the beginning of the interview, Natalia's friendliness put Stella at ease. She answered questions about the storm and the people in Royal, listing places that were badly damaged, giving facts and figures of families hit, the people who died in the storm and the enormous cost of the cleanup.

"If people would like to help, do you have an address?" Natalia asked.

"Yes," Stella replied, giving the address of the bank in Royal where the account had been set up for donations. "Also, the Texas Cattleman's Club of Royal will have a Christmas festival and we hope to be able to provide toys for all the children of families who were so badly hurt by the storm. Some families lost everything—their homes, their livestock, their livelihoods—and we want to help them have a happy holiday," Stella said, smiling into the camera before turning to Natalia.

Before Stella knew it, her fifteen-minute segment was finished.

When the show ended, Natalia turned to Stella. "Thank you. You gave a wonderful presentation today that should get a big response."

"I enjoyed having a chance to do the show and to tell about our Christmas festival. I'm very excited about that and the joy it will bring."

"Maybe we can have someone from the Royal and the Dallas TCC be on our show soon to mention it again."

"That would be wonderful," Stella said.

Natalia got a text, which she scanned quickly. "We're getting donations. Your bank will be able to total them up and let you know. Congratulations on getting more help for Royal."

Stella smiled broadly, happy that the interview went well, hoping they did get a big response.

After thanking them, telling them goodbye and making arrangements to get a video of the interview, she was ready to go back to Dallas.

As she left the station, people who worked there

stopped to greet her and wish her success in helping her town.

Exhilarated, she saw Sid holding the door of the limo as she emerged from the building.

"I watched your interview in the bar down the block and two guys there said they would send some money to Royal. Way to go," he said, and she laughed, giving Sid a high five, which after one startled moment, he returned.

Sid drove to an upscale shopping area in that city. He parked in front of a redbrick shop with an ornate dark wood front door flanked by two huge white pots of red hibiscus and green sweet potato vines that trailed over the sides of the pots. To one side of the door a large window revealed an interior of subdued lighting and white and red furniture. The only identifying sign was on the window near the door. Small gold letters spelled out the name, Chez Cecilia.

Sid hopped out to open her door. "Here's my number. Just give me a call a few minutes before you want to be picked up and I'll be right here."

"Thanks, Sid," she said, wondering what Aaron had gotten her into. She went inside the shop—which had soft music playing in the background, thick area rugs, contemporary oil paintings on the walls and ornately framed floor-to-ceiling mirrors—and asked for Cecelia.

A tall, slender brunette appeared, smiling and extending her hand. "You must be Stella. I'm happy to meet you. Let me take your coat," she said, taking Stella's jacket and hanging it up. "Aaron has told me about you."

"That surprises me," Stella said, curious how Aaron knew Cecelia and the dress shop but not wanting to pry. She'd rather Aaron would tell her the things he wanted her to know.

"Surprised me, too. Aaron keeps his world to himself. From what he told me, I think I know what we should show you. Let's get you comfortable. I have a few things picked out. He said you have a dinner date tonight with some people who want to hear about Royal and the storm and how they can help."

"You're right."

"Now make yourself comfortable. Can I get you a soft drink? Coffee or tea? Ice water?"

"Ice water please," she said, thinking this whole excursion was ridiculous, a feeling that changed to dismay when Cecilia began to bring clothes out to show her.

"Just tell me what appeals to you and we'll set it aside for you to try on if you'd like."

Within minutes Stella felt in a daze. Nothing Cecilia brought out looked like anything Stella had ever worn. Necklines were lower; hemlines were higher. Skirts were tighter and material was softer. "Cecelia, I can't imagine myself in these," she said, looking at a green dress of clinging material that had a low-cut cowl neckline and a tight, straight skirt with a slit on one side. "These are so unlike me."

"You may be surprised how nice they'll look on you. These are comfortable dresses, too."

Her dazed feeling increased when she tried on the dresses she selected, yet when she looked in the mirror, she couldn't keep from liking them.

When she tried to stop shopping, Cecilia shook her head. "You need to select an elegant dress for evening. You need two suits. You should have a business dress. Aaron made this very clear and he'll come down and pick something out himself if you don't. You will not want him to do that. Aaron is not into shopping for dresses. Our clothing is tasteful and lovely, but he doesn't select what's appropriate for business unless I help him. Fortunately, he'll listen."

Even as Stella laughed, she was surprised and wondered how Cecelia knew this about Aaron. It hinted at more mysteries in his life before she knew him.

Stella tried on a red silk wool sleeveless dress with a low V-neck that she would have to grow accustomed to because she hadn't worn a dress like this one ever. "Cecilia, this isn't me."

"That's the point, Stella. Aaron wants you to have dresses that will help you present a certain image. From what Aaron has said, you're trying to get help for your town. Believe me, that dress will help you get people's attention. It's beautiful on you."

Stella laughed and shook her head. "Thank you. I feel as if I'm only half-dressed."

"Not at all. You look wonderful."

Stella shook her head and studied her image, which she barely recognized.

"Try it," Cecilia urged. "You don't want Aaron shopping for you."

"No, I don't." She sighed. "I'll take this one."

The next two were far too revealing and she refused. "I would never feel comfortable even though these are beautiful dresses."

The next was a black dress that had a high neck in front, but was backless as well as sleeveless.

She had to agree with Cecilia that she looked pretty in the dress, but she wondered whether she would ever really wear it.

"You should have this. It's lovely on you," Cecilia said. "I know Aaron would definitely like this one."

She felt like telling Cecilia that she was not buying the dresses to please Aaron, but she wondered if she would be fooling herself in saying that. She finally nodded and agreed to take it, because she had to agree that she looked nice in it.

Not until the business suits was she comfortable in the clothes she tried on. The tailored dark blue and black suits were plain and her type of clothing. Until she tried on blouses to go with them. Once again, it was low necklines, soft, clinging material—so different from her usual button-down collars and cotton shirts.

Finally she was finished and had all her purchases bagged and boxed. She was shocked to look at her watch and see that it was almost four.

Sid came in to pick her purchases up and load them into the limo as Stella thanked Cecelia and the two other women who worked in the shop. Finally she climbed into the limo to return to Aaron's to get ready for dinner with the oil and gas executives who were potential donors.

When she arrived, Aaron was waiting on the drive. After she stepped out of the limo, Aaron and Sid carried her purchases into the house.

When Sid left them, Aaron closed the back door and turned to take her into his arms. "We're supposed to meet the people we're having dinner with in less than two hours. These are the oil and gas executives I told you about."

"Thanks, for setting this up, Aaron."

"I'm glad to, and Cole has made some appointments with potential donors, as well. How was your mother?"

"Busy with her own life."

"Have you told her about your pregnancy?"

"No. She was very unhappy to learn she was going to be a grandmother when my sister had her first baby. I think Mom thought it aged her to suddenly become a grandmother. She's not close to her grandchildren and doesn't really like children in general. My mother is in her own world. To her, my news will not be good news."

"Thank heavens you don't take after her. She's missing out on one of the best parts of life," he said, surprising her that a single guy would express it that way.

"It'll take over half an hour to drive to the restaurant," he continued after a pause. "We better start getting ready. I need to shower and shave."

"In other words, I need to start getting ready now," she said, "because I want to shower."

"We can shower together."

"If we don't leave the house tonight," she said.

He smiled. "We can't afford to stand these people up so we'll get ready and shower separately. Maybe tomorrow we can be together. Cecelia said she thinks I'll like what you bought."

"I don't know myself when I look in the mirror. In those dresses the reflection doesn't look like me, but hopefully, we'll achieve the effect you expect. If not, you wasted a lot of money."

"I think it'll be worth every penny."

"So you better run along and let me get ready."

He nodded, his eyes focused intently on her as he looked at her mouth. She stepped away. "Bye, Aaron. See you shortly."

"Come here," he said, taking her hand and leading her out to the central hall. "See that first open door on the left? When you're ready, meet me there. I'll wait for you in the library."

"The library. Fine," she said.

"See you soon," he said, brushing a light kiss on her lips and leaving her. She went back to shower and dress in the tailored black suit she had bought earlier with an old blouse that had a high collar— an outfit that she could relax in and be comfortable.

When she was ready, she went to the library to meet Aaron, who was already there waiting. Dressed in a brown suit and dark brown tie, he looked as handsome as he always did. His gaze raked over her and he smiled.

"You look pretty," he said, crossing the room to her. "We have to go, but I know what I'd prefer doing."

"I definitely feel the same, but you're right about having to go."

"Before we do, there's something I want you to

have," he said, turning to walk to a chair and pick up a gift that she hadn't noticed before. Wrapped in silver paper, it had a blue silk ribbon tied around it and a big silk bow on top. "This is for you."

Surprised, she looked up at him. "It's not my birthday," she said quietly, startled he was giving her a present.

"You're carrying my baby. That's very special and I want to give you something that you'll always have to celebrate the occasion."

"Aaron, that is so sweet," she said, hugging and kissing him. She wondered about the depth of his feelings for her. He had to care to give her such gifts and do so much for her. As quickly as that thought came and went, another occurred to her—that the makeover and clothes benefited Royal. Was she just a means to an end with him? She looked at the present in her hands. This one was purely for her because of the baby—a sweet gesture, but it still didn't mean he had special feelings for her beyond her motherhood.

Finally she raised her head. "Thank you," she whispered.

"Look at your present," he said. "You don't even know what I'm giving you."

Smiling, she untied the bow and carefully peeled away the paper. She raised the lid to find a black velvet box. She removed it from the gift box, opened it and gasped. "Aaron!" she exclaimed as she looked at a necklace made of gold in the shape of small delicate oak leaves, each with a small diamond for a stem. There was a golden leaf and diamond bracelet to match. "These are beautiful." She looked up at him. "These are so gorgeous. Thank you." She stepped forward to kiss him. He held her in one strong arm and kissed her. In seconds the other arm circled her waist and he leaned over her, still kissing her.

"Want to wear them tonight?"

She looked at her suit. "Yes, I'd love to."

"I tried to get something that you can wear whether it's day or night—in other words, all the time."

"I love this necklace and bracelet. I love that you thought of me and wanted to do this," she said, smiling at him.

"Let me put it on you," he said, and she nodded.

In seconds he stepped back. "Hold out your wrist." When she did, he fastened the bracelet on her slender wrist and kissed her lightly. "We'll celebrate more tonight when we get back home. Stella, a baby is precious. It is a celebration and this is just a tiny token."

"It's more than a token and I'll treasure it always, Aaron. It's absolutely beautiful," she said, thrilled that he was that happy about the baby.

"I'm glad you feel that way."

She nodded. Touched, wishing things were different, she felt her emotions getting out of hand. Tears stung her eyes.

"Ready? Sid's waiting."

"Yes," she answered, turning toward the door. She wanted to wipe her eyes but didn't want Aaron to know she was crying. If only he loved her— then his gift would hold a deeper meaning for her.

Seven

That evening, Stella really wowed her dinner companions. She gave a talk similar to the one in Lubbock, showing pictures of the devastation in Royal, which she had on her iPad. By the time the evening was over, it looked promising that the oil and gas executives were going to publicize Royal's need for financial help and make a large donation. As she and Aaron left the restaurant, she breathed a sigh of relief that her efforts for the town were paying off.

Then they went back to Aaron's house to make love through the night. They were in the big bed in the guest bedroom where she was staying. She wore her necklace and bracelet through the night, but in the morning as Aaron held her in his arms, he touched the necklace lightly. "Put your necklace and bracelet away today. Just leave them here instead of taking them to the salon."

"Sure," she answered, smiling at him.

"Sid has the limo waiting," Aaron said. "Tonight, we're meeting television executives from here in Dallas. These people can do a lot, Stella. Tomorrow we'll fly to Austin. You have a lunch, an interview and a dinner there and then we fly back to Dallas for one more interview at noon on Friday."

"Don't say another word. You'll just stir up my nerves more than ever."

"You're doing great. I'll tell you again, relax and enjoy your day at the salon. You better go now. I'm going to the office and I'll see you tonight. It'll take all day at the salon and, afterward, Sid will take you to the restaurant. Just call me when you're on the way. I'll try to get there before you do. That way we'll be ahead of the people we're meeting, so we can just sit and talk until they get there."

"You're getting me into more things," she said,

holding a bag with her new dress and clothes that she would wear to dinner. Aaron grinned.

"You'll look back on all of this and be glad. I promise." He took her arm and they left, pausing while he locked up.

When they greeted her at the salon, she couldn't believe her day was turning out this way. It commenced with a massage. As she relaxed, she thought of the contrast with her life the first night after the tornado and how she had fallen into bed about four in the morning and slept two hours to get up and go back to work helping people.

She had her first manicure and first pedicure, which both seemed unnecessary. In the afternoon she had a facial. Following the facial, a salon attendant washed her hair and passed her over to the stylist to cut and blow-dry her hair. By the time she was done, Stella felt like a different woman. Instead of straight brown hair that fell halfway down her back, her hair was now just inches above shoulder length. It fell in a silky curtain that curled under, with slight bangs that were brushed to one side.

Next, a professional did her makeup and took time to show Stella how to apply it herself.

By late afternoon when she looked in the mirror, Stella couldn't recognize herself. She realized that she had so rarely ever tried makeup and then only lipstick that it gave her an entirely different appearance, although the biggest change was her hair.

The salon women gushed over the transformation that was amazing to her. Finally, she dressed for the evening.

"I really don't even know myself," she told the tall blonde named Gretchen at the reception desk.

"You look gorgeous. Perfect. The dress you brought is also perfect. We hope you love everything—your makeup, your hair and your nails."

She smiled at Gretchen. "I'll admit that I do," she said, pleased by the result and wondering what Aaron would think. "I've had the same hairdo since I was in college. It became a habit and it was easy. It's amazing how different I look," she said, turning slightly to look at herself in the mirror. The red silk dress fit her changing waistline; her old clothes were beginning to feel slightly tight in the waist because of her pregnancy.

She still wore her black wool coat and couldn't see any reason for a new coat. When she thanked them and left, Sid smiled at her as he held the limo door.

"You look great," he said appreciatively. "Mr. Nichols isn't going to know you."

"Thanks, Sid. I don't feel quite like me."

"Might as well make the most of it," he said, and grinned. "You'll turn heads tonight."

"You think? Sid, that would be a first," she admitted, laughing as she climbed into the limo and he closed the door.

Midafternoon Aaron went home to shower and change into a charcoal suit, a custom-made white dress shirt and a red tie. He returned to the office to spend the rest of the day catching up on paperwork. Just as he was ready to leave, he was delayed by a phone call. It only took a few minutes, but he guessed he might not get to the restaurant ahead of Stella, so he sent her a text.

He had received a call from the businessmen who'd had dinner with them last night, and they wanted to donate $20,000 to Royal's relief efforts, which he thought would be another boost to Stella's self-confidence. Aaron knew Stella hadn't faced the fact that she was filling in for the mayor as Royal's representative to the outside world even if it wasn't official. She was filling in and getting better at it all the time.

When he arrived at the restaurant, Aaron parked and hurried across the lot. He wanted to see what transformations they had made at the salon. Whatever they had done, he hoped the bun had disappeared for the evening.

The only people in the lobby besides restaurant employees in black uniforms were a couple standing, looking at a picture of a celebrity who had eaten at the restaurant. He didn't see any sign of Stella. The couple consisted of a tall, black-haired man and a beautiful woman half-turned toward him as she looked at the photograph.

He saw the maître d' and motioned to him to ask him about Stella. As the maître d' approached, Aaron glanced again at the woman. The man had walked away, and she was now standing alone. She was stunning in a red dress that ended at her knees, showing shapely long legs and trim ankles in high-heeled red pumps.

"Sir?" the maître d' asked.

"I'm supposed to meet someone here," he said. "Ms. Daniels."

"Aaron?"

He heard Stella's voice and looked up. The woman in red had turned to face him and he almost looked past her before he realized it was Stella. "She's here," he heard himself say to the maître d'. Aaron had expected a change, but not such a transformation that he didn't recognize her. Desire burst with white heat inside him as he walked over to her.

"I didn't even recognize you," he said, astounded and unable to stop staring at her. The temperature around him climbed. He tried to absorb the fact that this was Stella, because she had changed drastically. He was now looking at a stunning beauty.

"I told you long ago you might need to get your eyes checked," she said, smiling at him and making him feel weak in the knees. "Aaron, it's still me."

"You're going to knock them dead with your looks," he said without even thinking about it.

"I hope not," she said, laughing. "Aaron, you're staring."

"Damn straight, I'm staring. I can't recognize you."

"Get used to it. I'm really no different. I take it you like what you see," she prompted.

"Like? I'm bowled over. Stella, do you recognize yourself?"

"I'll admit it's quite a change. I have to get accustomed to my hair."

"You look fantastic. Wait right here," Aaron said and walked back to the maître d' to talk to him. After a moment, Aaron came back to take her arm. "Come with me," he said. The maître d' smiled at them and turned to lead the way.

"Aaron?" she asked, glancing at him.

"Just a moment, you'll see," he answered her unasked question.

The maître d' stopped to motion them through an open door. They entered an office with a desk covered by papers. The maître d' closed the door behind them.

"I asked where I could be alone with you for a few minutes. He's right outside the door should anyone want in this office."

"What on earth are we doing here?"

"I gave you a necklace and bracelet as a token of a celebration because you're carrying my baby, Stella. It's a relatively simple gold necklace and bracelet that you can wear in the daytime and wear often, which is what I wanted. To celebrate our baby, I also want you to have something very special, because this is a unique time in your life and mine. This present you can't wear as often, but you can wear it tonight," he said, handing her a flat package tied in another blue ribbon.

"You've given me a beautiful present. You didn't need to do this." Her blue eyes were wide as she studied him and then accepted the box. She untied the ribbon and opened the velvet box and gasped. "Aaron. Oh, my heavens. This is beautiful. It's magnificent."

He picked up a diamond necklace that sparkled in the light. "Turn around and I'll put it on," he said.

"I've never had anything like this. I feel as if I need a bodyguard to wear it." She turned and he fastened it around her slender throat, brushing a kiss on her nape, catching a scent that was exotic and new for Stella.

"You've got one—me. There," he said after a moment, turning her to face him, his gaze going over her features. Her blue eyes looked bigger than ever with thick lashes framing them. She didn't have on heavy makeup, just enough to alter her looks, but her hair was what had thrown him off.

And now her figure showed in the red dress, which fit a waistline that still was tiny. The diamonds glittered on her slender throat.

"You're beautiful, and that's an inadequate description. *Stunning* is more like it."

"Thank you. I'm glad you're pleased and thank you for doing this for me."

"Do you like the change?"

"After your reaction, yes, I do. It takes some getting used to. I sort of don't recognize myself, either."

They looked at each other and smiled. "I'd kiss you, but it would mess up that makeup."

"Wait until later."

"We better give the guy back his office. I just wanted a private moment to give the necklace to you."

"It's dazzling. I've never had anything like it."

He took her arm and they stepped out. "Thanks," Aaron said, slipping some folded bills to the maître d'. Then he turned to Stella and said, "Let's go meet your public. You'll wow them and get a bundle for Royal."

"Don't make me jittery," she said, but she

sounded far more sure of herself than she had on that first drive to Lubbock.

"Also, I didn't tell you. I got a text from the guys last night. They're sending a check to the Royal storm recovery fund for $20,000."

She turned to gaze at him with wide eyes. "Mercy, Aaron. That's a big amount."

"You just wait and see what you can do for your hometown." He glanced at the maître d'. "We're ready for our table now and you can show the others in when they arrive."

Aaron introduced her to two men and a woman, all executives of a television station. Through salads and dinner Stella told them stories of people affected by the storm. Over dessert, and after-dinner drinks for everyone except Stella, she showed them her presentation on her iPad.

"Stella has suggested a Christmas drive," Aaron said, "to get presents for those who lost everything, for families with children and people still in the hospital."

"That's a wonderful idea," the woman, Molly Vandergrift, said. "I think that would be a great general-interest story. Would you like to appear on our news show and talk about this?"

"I'd love to," Stella replied, meaning it, realizing she was losing the butterflies in her stomach. Along with the change in her appearance and the money that she had already raised, she was gaining more confidence in her ability to talk to people about Royal. And tonight, the three television executives were so friendly, enthusiastic and receptive that she felt even better.

"We're going to try to tie it into the Texas Cattleman's Club Christmas festival in Royal this year," she added.

"That'll be good to have on a show. I know Lars West with the Dallas TCC. We could get him to come on, too, with Stella. Are the TCC here doing anything?"

"They will," Aaron replied. "I've just started talking to them."

"I'm sure the sooner you can do this, the better. I'll send a text now," Molly said, "and see if we can get you on the Friday show."

"That would be grand," Stella answered. "Everyone in Royal will appreciate what you're doing to help." She was aware Aaron had been quieter all evening than he had been in Lubbock, letting her do most of the talking. When she glanced at him, he looked pleased.

Excitement hummed in her because she was going to get so much support for Royal. As the evening wore on, she was even more pleased with her makeover, relieved that she could begin to relax talking to people and enjoy meeting them.

They didn't break up until after ten o'clock. She and Aaron told them goodbye outside as valets brought the cars to the door.

Finally she was alone in Aaron's car with him. He drove out of the lot, but on the drive back, he pulled off the road slightly, put the car in Park and turned to kiss and hug her. Then he leaned away. "You were fantastic tonight. No butterflies either—right?"

"I think they're gone," she said.

"They'll never come back, either. Awesome evening. You did a whiz-bang job. Watch. The television show will be wonderful for Royal."

"I think so, too," she said, feeling bubbly and excited. "Thanks, Aaron, for all you've done for me. And thank you again for this fabulous necklace that I was aware of all evening."

"You're welcome. Stella, you'll be able to do more and more for Royal."

"I hope so." As he drove home they discussed the evening and what they would do Friday.

The minute they were in the kitchen of his house, Aaron turned her. "You take my breath away," he said.

Her heart skipped a beat as she gazed at him. "Thank you again for the diamonds. They're beautiful."

"That's why I didn't want you to take your gold necklace for tonight. I had something else in mind." He slipped his arms around her and kissed her, his tongue thrusting deeply as he held her. After a while he raised his head. "Go with me to the TCC Christmas festival. Will you?"

"I'd be delighted, thank you," she replied.

He kissed her again, picking her up to carry her to the guest bedroom where she was staying. Still kissing her, he stood her on her feet by the bed. "I can't stop looking at you," he whispered. He drew her to him to kiss her. When he released her, he slid the zipper down the back of her dress and pushed it off her shoulders. As it fell around her feet, he leaned back to look at her. "You changed everything," he said.

"I bought the underwear when I purchased the dress," she said as he unfastened the clasp of the lacy red bra that was a wisp of material and so different from her usual practical cotton underwear.

He placed his hands on her hips and inhaled deeply. "You're gorgeous," he whispered, his eyes raking over her lacy panties down to her thigh-high stockings. She was still in her red pumps.

As he looked at her she unfastened the buttons of his shirt and pushed it off his shoulders. Her hands worked to loosen his belt and then his suit trousers and finally they fell away and she pushed down his briefs to free him.

She stroked him lightly and he inhaled, picking her up. She kicked off her pumps, and he placed her on the bed, switching on a small bedside light before kneeling beside her to shower her with kisses.

As she wound her arms around his neck, she rose up slightly, pulling him to her to kiss him. "Aaron, this is so good," she whispered.

He moved over her, kissing her passionately while she clung to him.

Later, she lay in his arms, held closely against him. "Aaron, you're changing my life."

He shifted on his side to face her, toying with locks of her hair. "You're changing mine, too, you know."

"I suppose," she said, gazing solemnly into his eyes. "I hadn't thought about that, but I guess a baby will change both of us. Even just knowing we'll have a baby will bring changes. I was talking about this week and my makeover, my new clothes, meeting so many people and persuading them to help. Of course, I have the pictures and figures to persuade them."

"You're the cause, more than pictures and numbers. The mayor couldn't have had anyone do a better job." Aaron wound his fingers in her hair.

"It's a long time from now, but do you think you'll be present when our baby is born?"

"I want to be and I hope you want me to be there," he said.

"Yes, I do," she answered, hurting, wishing she had his love. "I want you to be there very much."

He hugged her again. "Then that's decided. I'll

be there." They became silent and she wondered if he would still feel the same way when their baby came into the world.

"You're beautiful, Stella," Aaron said hoarsely. He drew her closer against him. "I don't want to let you go," he whispered as his arms tightened around her.

Her face was pressed against his chest and she hugged him in return. "I don't want you to let me go ever," she whispered, certain it was so soft, he couldn't hear her. "Tonight we have each other," she said. "Tomorrow we go home and back to the problems."

When they flew back to Royal on Saturday afternoon, she had eight more big checks to deposit in the Royal storm recovery fund. As they sat in the plane, she was aware of Aaron studying her. "What?" she asked. "You're staring."

"I'm thinking about all the changes in you. Now you'll be the talk of Royal with your makeover, plus the money you're bringing in to help everyone."

She laughed. "I'll be the talk of Royal maybe for five minutes. But the checks will last for quite a while. Aaron, I'm so thrilled over the money. People have been really generous. Thank for your introductions."

"Thanks, Stella, for talking to all of them. You're doing a fantastic job. As for the talk of the town—it'll be longer than five minutes. I suspect some guys are going to ask you out. I think I should make my presence known."

She was tempted to fling *What do you care?* at him. How much did he care? He acted as if he wanted to be with her. He had done so much for her—in the long run, the results had been for Royal, so she didn't know how much of his motivation came from feelings for her or if it was for the town. Even the jewelry had been for her because she was having his baby—not necessarily because he loved her for herself.

She didn't know any more about what he felt now than she had after their first night together.

The sex was fabulous, but did it mean deeper feelings were taking root with Aaron or was it still simply lust and a good time?.

Aaron would talk to Cole Saturday or Sunday and then she would know if the TCC had made any more decisions about the Christmas festival. It could be so much fun for everyone if they opened it up for all to attend.

She hoped to get into her town house soon and have her own little Christmas tree. Each day she was in Royal, she noticed more trees going up in various places in town. Some Christmases they had had a decorated tree on the lawn of the town hall. She wanted to ask about putting up a Christmas tree on the town-hall lawn this year because she hated for the storm to destroy any customs they had.

"You have appointments for us starting Monday with a lunch in Austin and dinner that night. The next day we go to Houston and Wednesday, we have a noon meeting in Dallas. We won't be back to Royal until after lunch Wednesday. No more until after Christmas, Aaron. I need to be in Royal so I can focus on the Christmas gift drive."

"You'll be back Wednesday afternoon. Then you can start catching up."

After landing she ate with Aaron at the Cozy Inn, sitting and talking until after ten. At the door to her suite, she glanced at him as she inserted the card in the slot. "Want to come in?"

"I thought you'd never ask," he said. He held the door for her and she entered.

She turned to face him. "Want something to drink?"

He walked up to her and pulled her close. "No, thank you. I want you in my arms."

She kissed him, wrapping her arms around his narrow waist, holding him, wondering if they were forging any kind of lasting bond at all.

After appearing in Austin for a TV interview on Monday, they flew to Houston on Tuesday. During the flight, Stella turned to Aaron. He was dressed to meet people as soon as they landed. He had shed his navy suit jacket and loosened his matching tie. He sat across from her with his long legs stretched out in the roomy private jet.

She was comfortable in her new navy suit and matching silk blouse. She, too, had shed her suit jacket.

"Still no morning sickness?" he asked.

"Not at all," she said. "Aaron, I've had three job offers this week."

His eyebrows arched. "Oh? Who wants to hire you?"

"The Barlow Group in Houston. They want me

for vice president of public relations. It's a prestigious Texas foundation that raises money for
good causes."

"I know who you're talking about. I have a
friend on their board. Who else has made an
offer?" he asked, frowning slightly as he waited.

"A Dallas charity—Thompkins Charities, Ltd.
They also want me for director of public relations."

"Another prestigious group that does a lot of
good. That's old oil money. I have several friends
there."

"The third one is No Hungry Children in Dallas
who want me for a coordinator-of-services position. The only one I'm considering is the Barlow
Group in Houston. I'm seriously thinking about
taking that job. It pays more than I make now. It
would be in Houston, which would be nice. I can
help a lot of people—that would be my dream
career."

"Congratulations on the offers. Frankly, you're
needed in Royal, though."

"Royal is beginning to mend. They can get
along without me."

"People have talked to me and I think the whole

town wants you to step in and become acting mayor."

"I definitely don't think it's the whole town. The town council would be the ones to select someone and they haven't said a word to me. I can't imagine the town really wanting me for that role."

"Wednesday we're going back to Royal. Are you moving out of the Cozy Inn Friday?"

"Yes. My town house is all fixed up, so I'm going home. Friday or Saturday I'm getting a Christmas tree and decorating it."

"I have appointments Thursday in Royal and Friday I have to go to Dallas. I hate to leave now, but this is a deal I've worked on since before the storm hit. A wealthy family from back east wants to move to Dallas and build a new home. He was a college buddy, so there is a personal interest. I made a bid for R&N on building it. Now they've finally decided to go with R&N Builders. It's a five-million-dollar house, so I have to see them and be there to sign the contract. Cole could, but that would take him away from Royal and this is really something I've dealt with and I know the family."

"Aaron, go to Dallas," she said, smiling. "That's simple enough."

"That's what I have to do. I just wanted you to know why. I still can move you in early Friday morning before I go to Dallas. Also, I'll help you get a tree on Saturday if you'd like."

"I'd like your help on the tree," she said, smiling at him. "I don't have a lot to move, so I can move home all by myself. Will you stay in Royal through Christmas and New Year's?"

"Yes. Probably about January 3, I'll go back to Dallas for a little while. I'll still be back and forth."

That thought hurt. She would miss him, but she had known that day was inevitable.

Sadness gripped her and she tightened her fist in her lap. "Next week is the TCC Christmas festival. It should be so much fun, Aaron. We're getting lots of presents and I haven't been there this week, but I've had texts from Lark, from Paige and from Megan Maguire."

"You're right—it will be fun. You'll be shocked by the number of presents that are coming into the TCC. That doesn't count the ones dropped off at businesses, fire stations, all over town."

"We have envelopes with checks for individuals and families that are on our list. I'm so grateful we've been able to do this."

"The Christmas drive is a great idea," he said.

She smiled. "Right now I'm excited over the Christmas festival," she said, thinking it would be another chance for her to spend time with Aaron. When January came and he returned to Dallas, it was going to be hard on her without him. She knew that, but she pushed aside her fears. Friday she would move out of the Cozy Inn. She would never again see it without thinking of Aaron.

Their pilot announced they were approaching the Houston area.

"This is exciting, Aaron. I hope we can raise a lot of money and get more help for Royal," she said, slipping into her suit jacket.

By Wednesday afternoon they had finished the interviews, the dinners, the talks to groups, and were flying back to Royal. Aaron knew some money had been sent directly to Royal, some checks had been given to Stella and some to him. He sat with a pen and pad in hand figuring out a rough total. She remained quiet.

When he raised his head, he smiled. "You've done a wonderful job, Stella. As far as the money, the checks that have been promised and the ones we're taking back with us total approximately a quarter of a million dollars. That's tremendous. I don't think the mayor himself could have done any better."

"I'm just astounded by the help we've received. Some of it was from out-of-state people seeing interviews that got picked up and broadcast nationally. I can't believe I've had three more offers to go on television news and local interest shows after the first of the year."

"You look good on camera."

She laughed. "Don't be ridiculous. That isn't why I'm asked."

"I think that's a big part of it."

"I'm sure that it's much more because Royal has some touching stories."

"They do, but it helps to have a pretty lady tell them."

Shaking her head at him, she changed the topic. "I'm hungry and ready to get my feet on the ground in Royal and have dinner."

"That's easy. Where would you like to eat? I'll take you wherever you'd like to go?"

"After being gone this week, I'm happy to eat at the inn."

"That suits me."

"Good," she answered, certain their lives would change and wondering if Aaron would leave hers.

"We'll be on the ground now in about thirty minutes," he said, and she looked out the window, glad to get back to Royal and home.

"It'll be my last two nights in the Cozy Inn," she said, thinking how soon Aaron would be leaving the hotel, too.

"Stella, would you like for me to go with you to a doctor's appointment?"

"I've got to find a doctor in Royal. I went to Houston to my sister's doctor, but I want a doctor here."

"Definitely. I'd like to go with you and meet the doctor."

"I think that would be nice. I'll ask about a pediatrician here, too. I don't want to drive to Dallas each time I need to see the doctor."

"No, you shouldn't. I'll make arrangements for

our plane to take you to Dallas when you need to go, but I think you should have a doctor here."

"Thanks, Aaron. I'm glad you're interested."

"Stella, you'd be surprised if you knew how deep my interest runs. You and this baby are important to me," he said in a serious tone and with a somber look in his brown eyes. Her heart skipped. How much did he really mean that? He had included her with the baby. She figured that he had an interest in his child, but she had no idea of the depth of his feelings for her.

How important was she to him?

Stella went by the hospital Thursday. A doctor was with Mayor Vance, so she couldn't see him. She talked briefly with his wife and found out he was still improving, so Stella said she would come back in a few days. She called on others and talked to Lark briefly about the Christmas drive.

Lark smiled at her. "Stella, I really didn't recognize you at first. Your hair is so different and it changes your whole appearance. I saw you on a Dallas TV show. You were great and you took our case to a big audience. It's wonderful for people here to find out about these agencies and how to access them."

"Some of those agencies were new to me. I didn't know all that help was available."

"The shows should do a lot for us. You got in a plug for the Christmas drive also, which was nice. Speaking of the drive, I think there will be some big presents for people this Christmas."

"I hope so. Some of the stores are donating new TV sets for each family on our list. That'll be a fun present. Other stores are sending enough iPads for each family to have one. It makes me feel good to be able to help. I hope Skye and the baby are getting along."

"We just take everything one day at a time for both of them. There's still no word on Jacob Holt. If you hear anything, please call."

"I will, I promise. I'm home to stay now until Christmas Eve day when I'll go to my sister's."

"You just look beautiful. I love your hair."

"Thanks. You're nice."

"I have a feeling your quiet nights at home that you talk about are over," Lark said, smiling at her.

Stella laughed. "I'll keep in touch on the Christmas drive."

As she left the hospital, outside on the sidewalk, she heard someone call her name. She turned to see Cole headed her way.

"Hey, you look great."

"Thanks, Cole." To her surprise, he smiled at her. Since the storm she had rarely seen Cole smile.

"You're doing a bang-up job for the town. Aaron has let me know. Excellent job."

"Thanks. I'm glad to and I'm thrilled by people's generosity and finding specific agencies that can meet people's needs."

"I just wanted to thank you. See you around."

"That's nice, Cole."

He headed toward the hospital entrance and she wondered whom he was going to see. There were still too many in the hospital because of the storm over two months later.

"Stella, wait up."

She turned to see Lance Higgens, a rancher from the next county and someone she had known most of her life. She smiled at him, feeling kindly because the afternoon of the tornado he had come to Royal to help and that night he had made a $1,000 donation to the relief effort.

"I saw you on television yesterday."

"Good. I guess a lot of people caught that show around here."

"I didn't recognize you until they introduced you. You look great and you did a great job getting attention for Royal. I'd guess you'll get some donations."

"We did, Lance," she said. "We received one right away."

"Good. Listen, there's a barn dance at our town center next Saturday night. Would you like to go with me?"

Startled, she smiled at him. "I'm sorry, I'm going to a dinner that night, but thanks for asking me, Lance. That's very nice."

"Sure. Maybe some other time," he said. "Better go. Good to see you, Stella."

"Good to see you, too," she said, wanting to laugh. He had never looked at her twice before, never asked her to anything even though they had gone through high school together.

Her next stop was the drugstore where she ran into Paige. "Stella!" Paige called, and caught up with her.

"You never come to town. What are you doing here again?" Stella asked, smiling at her friend.

"I didn't plan well for anything this week. I saw you on television yesterday. Word went around that you'd be on—probably thanks to Aaron. You look fantastic and you did a great job. I love your makeover except I hardly know you."

"Thanks. It's the same me."

"Actually, I didn't even recognize you at first glimpse."

"Frankly, I barely recognize myself. The makeover has been fun and brought a bit of attention."

Paige's eyes narrowed. "I'll bet you're getting asked out by guys who never have asked you before."

Stella could feel her cheeks grow hot. "A little," she admitted. "I suppose looks are important to guys."

"Stella, most girls come to that conclusion before they're five years old," Paige remarked, and they both laughed. "We need a brief meeting soon for our Christmas drive to figure out how to coordinate the last-minute details. It's almost here."

"If you have a few minutes," Stella said, "we can go across the street to the café and talk about the drive now."

"Sure. Now's as good a time as any," Paige said.

"We're running out of time. Christmas is one week away and the TCC festival is next Tuesday."

They walked to Stella's car, where she picked up her notebook. Then they crossed the street to a new café that had opened since the storm. As soon as they were seated, Stella opened the binder with notes and lists.

"Presents and donations are pouring in and I can add to them with checks I brought back from my talks this week."

"That's fantastic. I'll be there that night and I'll check with the others so we can help pass out envelopes with checks and help people get their presents. I'm sure some of the TCC guys will pitch in."

"I really appreciate all you're doing. I think we've contacted everyone we should and there's been enough publicity that no one will be overlooked. We'll have money or gifts for all the people who've lost so much and lost a loved one—I'm sorry, Paige, to bring that up with you," Stella said.

"It's the reality of life. So many of us live with loss. Lark's sister in a coma, Cole's lost his brother, Henry Markham lost a brother—you know the list. Holidays are tough for people with any big loss—that doesn't have to be because of the tornado—people like Aaron. I suppose that's why he's so sympathetic toward Cole."

"Aaron?"

Paige's gray eyes widened. "Aaron's wife and child."

Stella stared at Paige. "Aaron lost a wife and child?" she repeated, not thinking about how shocked she sounded.

"Aaron hasn't told you? You didn't know that?" Paige asked, frowning. "I thought that was general knowledge. It happened years ago. Maybe I know more about Aaron because of his connection to Cole and Craig."

Stella stared into space, stunned by Paige's revelation. "He's never told me," she said, talking more to herself than Paige. She realized Paige had asked her a question and looked at her. "I'm sorry. What did you say?"

"I'm surprised he hasn't told you. I've always known— Cole and I went to the service. A lot of people in Royal knew. I think his baby was a little over a year old. The little boy and Aaron's wife were killed in a traffic accident. It was sudden—one of those really bad things. He's been single since then. It was six or seven years ago. A long time. I don't think he's dated much since, but I know the two of you have been together. I figured that's because of the storm."

"He doesn't talk about his private life or his past and I don't ask. I figure he'll tell me what he wants me to know."

"Men don't talk about private things as much. Aaron may be one of those who doesn't talk at all. I know at one point Craig said Aaron was having a tough time dealing with his loss."

"Paige, I just stayed at his house in Dallas this week. I didn't see any pictures of a wife and child."

"He may not have any. That wouldn't occur to some men."

"Maybe. I also wasn't all over the house. I was just in the back part and the guest bedroom. We didn't even eat there."

"Well, then, it would be easy to not see any pictures. Especially if he has a big house like Cole. Sorry if finding out about his wife and child upset you."

"Oh, don't be silly. It's common knowledge as

you said. I'm glad to know. He's just never talked to me about it. It does explain some things about him. Well, back to this Christmas drive—" Stella said, trying for now to put Aaron and his past out of her thoughts and concentrate on working out last-minute details of the event with Paige.

They worked another fifteen minutes before saying goodbye. Stella watched Paige walk away, a slender, willowy figure with sunlight glinting on her auburn hair, highlighting red strands.

Stella sat in the car, still stunned over Aaron's never mentioning his loss. Now she had the explanation for the barrier he kept between himself and others, the door he closed off when conversations or situations became too personal.

No wonder he held back about personal relationships—he was still in love with his late wife. And he'd lost his baby son. That's why babies were so special to him. Stella was unaware of the tears running down her cheeks. She had to stop seeing so much of Aaron. She couldn't cut him out of her life completely because of their baby, but she saw no future in going out with him. She didn't want to keep dating, because she was falling more deeply in love with him all the time while his emotions, love and loyalties were still back with the wife and child he had lost. She was glad he loved them, but he should have leveled with her.

Tears fell on the back of her hand and she realized she was crying. "Aaron, why didn't you tell me?" she whispered. If he really loved her, he would have shared this hurt with her, shared that very private bit of himself. Love didn't cut someone off and shut them out.

She wiped her hand and got a tissue to dry her eyes and her cheeks. Knowing she would have to pay attention to her driving, she focused on the car lot as she turned the key in the ignition.

She drove to the Cozy Inn and stepped out of the car, gathering packages to take inside. She hoped she didn't see Aaron before she reached her suite. She wanted to compose herself, think about what she would say.

She would have to make some decisions about her life with Aaron.

She would see him tonight at dinner. Once again her life was about to change. The sad part was that she would have to start to cut Aaron out of it and see far less of him.

Stella was tempted to confront him with the

information she'd learned and ask why he hadn't told her, but instead she wanted him to tell her voluntarily without her asking about it. There was no way she would accept his marriage proposal when he didn't even trust her enough to tell her something that vital. And if he still loved his first wife with all his heart, Stella didn't want to marry him.

Sadly, he wasn't ready to marry again—at least not for love. He had to love his late wife and child enormously still, maybe to the point of being unable to let go and face that they had gone out of his life forever.

Deep inside, her feelings for him crashed and shattered.

Eight

For their dinner tonight, Stella wore one of her new sweaters—a pale blue V-neck—and black slacks. She wore his gold-leaf necklace and bracelet but fought tears when she put the jewelry on.

She went to meet him, her body tingling at the sight of him while eagerness tinged with sadness gripped her as she crossed the Cozy Inn lobby. Aaron was in a black sweater, jeans and boots. She really just wanted to walk into his embrace, but she had to get over even wanting to do so.

"You're gorgeous, Stella. I've missed seeing you all day."

She smiled at him as he took her arm. As soon as they were seated, she picked up a menu.

After they ordered and were alone, he looked at her intently, his gaze slowly traveling over her. "I can't get used to the change in you. I've seen women change hairdos, men shave their heads and grow mustaches, a lot of things that transform appearances, but yours is the biggest change I've ever seen. I never expected you to change this much. It's fabulous."

"Thank you," she said, beginning to wonder if he would lose interest if she returned to looking the way she always had. The minute she thought about it, she remembered that it wouldn't matter because she was going to see him less often.

"Several people have called to thank me for getting you on television because they've found the agency they need for help."

"Good," she said. It was the first bright bit of news since she had sat down to dinner with him.

"Club members have been getting word out that the entire town is invited to the TCC Christmas festival, so I think we will have a big turnout."

"That is wonderful," she said. "It should be a happy time for people," she said. "For a little while that evening, maybe they can all forget their

losses and celebrate the season. I know it's fleet-
ing, but it's better than nothing."

"It's a lot better than nothing. It will help people
so much and kids will have a great time. Some
of the women are beginning to plan games and
things they can do for the kids. It'll be an evening
to look back on when we all pulled together and
had a great time."

"That's good," she said, and then thought of
his loss, sorry that Christmas was probably a bad
time for Aaron.

She felt responsible for him staying in Royal for
the holidays. She didn't think he would be if she
hadn't talked about how it would help others if he
would stay and do things for people who needed
something at holiday time.

She didn't want to deliberately hurt him. But it
had ended between them as far as she was concerned. She had to get over him even though she
had fallen in love with him.

How long would it take her to get over Aaron?

"Did you buy a dress for the Christmas festival?" he asked.

"Aaron, I already had a dress," she said, beginning to wonder if he was wound up in her new

persona and really didn't have that much interest in the former plain Jane that she was. It was
a little annoying. Was he not going to like her if
she reverted to her former self? She suspected it
didn't matter, because after the Christmas festival she didn't expect to continue the intimate relationship they had. She would see him because of
their baby, but it would be a parental relationship
and not what they had now. She might be with
him a lot where their child was concerned, but
they wouldn't be having an affair and she wasn't
going to marry a man who was still in love with
his deceased wife. Aaron couldn't even talk to her
about his wife and baby, so he hadn't let go at all.

"I think you should have something new and
special," he said, breaking into her thoughts.

"Don't go shopping for a dress for me," she said.
"I have a new dress for the festival I got at Cecilia's shop."

Three people stopped by their table to talk to
her and tell her what a great job she had done on
television Saturday. As the third one walked away,
Aaron smiled at her. "I can see the butterflies are
completely gone to another home."

"Yes, they are. Thanks to you."

"No, Stella. You did that yourself. You're the one who's developed poise to deal with people. You're the one who's talking to people, telling them what happened, telling people here how to get help. Oh, no. This isn't me. It's you. You have more confidence now and you're handling things with more certainty. You've brought about the changes in yourself. Maybe not hair and makeup, but confidence and self-assurance, making some of the tough decisions that have to be made about who gets help first. No, this is something you've done yourself."

"Thanks for the vote of confidence."

"I've had several people ask me if I would talk to you about stepping in as acting mayor. They're going to have to find someone soon."

"Now *that* position I'm not qualified for," she said firmly.

"Of course, you are. You're already doing the job. Take a long look at yourself," he said, and his expression was serious, not the cocky friendliness that he usually exhibited.

"I see an administrative assistant."

"Look again, Stella. The administrative assistant disappeared the afternoon of the storm.

You're all but doing Mayor Vance's job now. And I checked. The role will end before you have your baby next summer, so that won't be a problem."

She was thinking half about the job and half about Aaron, who looked incredible. How was she going to break things off with him?

All she had to do was remember than he had not recovered from his loss enough to even talk about it. He could not love anyone else and she hadn't changed her views of marrying without love. She wasn't going to do it.

They ate quietly. She listened to him talk about Royal and the things that had happened in the past few days. Finally, he leaned back in his chair, setting down his glass of water while he gazed at her.

"You're quiet. You've hardly said two words through dinner."

"Part of it was simply listening to you and learning what happened while we were in Dallas. I'm worn-out from the whirlwind week coming on top of everything else I've been doing."

"I think it's more than that. You weren't this quiet yesterday."

They stared at each other and she then looked down at her lap. "Aaron, tomorrow I move back to my town house. We have the festival coming up and we're going together. I want to get through that without any big upsets in my life."

"Why do I feel I'm part of what might be a big upset in your life? I don't see how I can be, but I don't think you'd be so quiet with me if I wasn't."

"I think it would be better if we talk when we're upstairs. This really isn't the place."

"I'd say that's incentive to get going," he said. "Are you ready?"

"Yes," she said. When she stood up, he held her arm lightly and led her from the dining room, stopping to say something to the maître d' and then rejoining her.

At her door to her suite, she invited him inside. When they were in the living room, she turned to face him. "What would you like to drink?"

He shook his head as he closed the space between them. He drew her close to kiss her. She melted into his arms, her heart thudding as she kissed him. She wound her arms around him to hold him close, kissing him in return, her resolutions nagging while she ignored them to kiss him.

She ran her fingers in his short, thick hair at the back of his head. She didn't want to stop kissing.

She wanted him in her bed all night long. She thought about his loss and knew she couldn't keep spending days and nights with him or she would be so hopelessly in love she would be unable to say no to him.

Finally she stepped back. Both of them were breathing hard. She felt a tight pang and wanted him badly. Just one more night—the thought taunted her. It was tempting to give in, to step back into his arms and kiss him and forget all the problems.

In the long run, it would be better to break it off right now. She wouldn't be hurt as much. She didn't think he would ever love anyone except the first wife. It had been long enough for him to adjust to his loss better than he had. No one ever got over it, they just learned to deal with it and go on with life.

She could imagine how desperately he wanted this baby after losing his first one. She suspected before long he would start showering her with more presents and pressuring her to marry him— and it would be because of their baby.

She would be glad to have him in their baby's life, but that was where it would have to stop. She couldn't go into a loveless marriage just to please Aaron.

She stared at him, making sure she had his attention and he wasn't thinking about kissing her again. "I can't do this, Aaron. We're not wildly in love. I think this is a purely physical relationship. Frankly, it's lust. If we keep it up, I might fall in love with you."

"So what's wrong with that picture," he said, frowning and placing one hand on his hip.

"Because I don't think you're going to fall in love. This is a physically satisfying relationship that you can walk away from at any point in time. Emotionally, you're not in it. I don't want that. I don't want to be in love with a man who isn't in love with me in return."

"I might fall in love and I think we've been good together, and I think I've been good with you and to you, Stella."

"You've been fantastic and so very good to me. I don't want to stop seeing you, I just want to back off and take a breather from the heavy sex. That isn't like me and I can't do that without my emotions getting all entangled."

His frown disappeared and he stepped closer to

place one hand lightly on her hip. "I can back off. Are you going to still let me kiss you?"

His question made her feel ridiculous. "As if I could stop you."

"I don't use force," he said as he leaned forward to brush a light kiss on her lips. "Okay, so we don't go to bed together. You'll set the parameters and send me home when you want me to go. In the meantime, kisses are good. Don't cut me off to the point where we don't even have a chance to fall in love," he whispered as he brushed kisses on her throat, her ear, the corner of her mouth.

She should have been more firm with him, but when he started talking, standing so close, his eyes filled with desire, his voice lowering, coaxing—she couldn't say no or tell him to leave. She would have to sometime during the night, but not for a few minutes. There wasn't any point in ending seeing him before Christmas, because they were going to be thrown together constantly and she didn't want a pall hanging over them.

And she couldn't ever end it entirely because of their baby.

His kiss deepened as his arms tightened around her, holding her against him. He was aroused, kissing her passionately, and she stopped thinking and kissed him in return.

Finally he picked her up. She was about to protest when he sat in the closest chair and held her on his lap, but ended up forgetting her protest and wrapping her arms around his neck to continue kissing him. How was she going to protect her heart?

His hand went beneath her sweater to caress her and in minutes he had both hands on her. When he slipped her sweater over her head, she caught his wrists, taking her sweater from him to pull it on again and slide off his lap.

"Aaron, let's say good-night," she said, facing him as she straightened her sweater.

"This is really what you want?" he asked.

"Tonight, it is. I need some space to think and sort out things."

He nodded. "Sure. Maybe you just need some time off. It's been a great week, Stella. You've done so much. You've been a great representative for Royal."

"Thanks. Thanks for everything," she whispered, scared she would cry or tell him to stay for the night or, worse, walk back into his arms, which was what she wanted.

"See you in the morning, hon," he said, brushing a kiss on her cheek and leaving.

She closed the door behind him and touched her cheek with her hand while tears spilled over. She loved him and this was going to be hard. After Christmas she would break up with him. But she wasn't ruining Christmas for either one of them. Suppose she had a little boy who looked like Aaron and was a reminder of his daddy every day of his life?

She had expected Christmas to be so wonderful. Instead, she was beginning to wonder how she would get through it

"Aaron," she whispered, knowing she was in love. He had been so good to her, helping her in multiple ways, changing her life, really. He was a good guy, honorable, loyal, fun to be with, sexy, loving. Was she making a mistake sending him away? Should she live with him and hope that someday he would love her? Was not telling her about his family an oversight—did he think she already knew because so many did?

She doubted it. She thought it was what gave

him the shuttered look, what caused him to throw up an invisible barrier. He still had his heart shut away in memories and loss and she couldn't reach it, much less ever have his love.

Aaron lay in bed in the dark, tossing and turning, his thoughts stormy. He missed Stella. He wanted to make love to her, wanted just to be with her. It was obvious something was bothering her. Why wouldn't she just tell him and let them work it out?

Had it been the gifts? Did she want an engagement ring, instead?

He had proposed that first night he learned she was pregnant, but she had turned him down and she would until he declared he loved her and made a commitment to her with his whole heart. Without talking about it, he knew she was bothered and scared she was falling in love and he wouldn't love her in return.

He liked her and maybe there was love up to a point, but he wasn't into making a total commitment to her. He couldn't tell her he loved her with his whole heart and that was what she wanted to hear. They hadn't talked about it, but he felt he was right.

He enjoyed being with her more than any other woman since Paula. It surprised him to realize he wasn't thinking as often of Paula. He would always love her and Blake and always miss them. He knew every time February 5 came around that it would have been Blake's birthday. It always hurt and it always would.

All the more reason he wanted Stella in his life—because this baby was his and he wasn't losing his second child. All he had to do was tell Stella he loved her with his whole heart. But he couldn't; he had to be truthful about it. He was trying to back off and give her room, let her think things through. Why wouldn't she settle for what they had, which was very good. They might fall in love in time and he might be able to handle his loss better. But that wasn't good enough for Stella, because she wouldn't take a chance on falling in love later.

Stella had some strong beliefs and held to them firmly.

Tossing back the covers, he got out of bed. This was his first night away from her for a little while, and he was miserable. What would he feel like in

January when they parted for maybe months at a time?

Aaron felt caged in the small suite at the Cozy Inn. At home he would just go to his gym and work out hard enough that he had to concentrate on what he was doing until he was so exhausted he would welcome bed and sleep. Even without her. He couldn't do that here. Knowledge that she was sleeping nearby disturbed him. He could go to her easily, but she would just say no.

Stella was intelligent. He figured at some point she would see they were compatible, the sex was fantastic and she surely would see that, hands down, it would be best for her baby to have a daddy—a daddy who would love him or her and be able to provide well for all of them.

Then he thought about Stella's makeover. He had heard enough talk—guys in Royal had asked her out since she had been back in town after their first trip to Dallas. Trey Kramer had even asked Aaron if they were dating because he wanted to ask her out if she wasn't committed. That didn't thrill him. He had told Trey that he was dating Stella, but when he returned to work in Dallas in

January, Aaron expected her to be asked out often by several men.

The thought annoyed him. He didn't want to think about her with other men and he didn't want the mother of his child marrying another man. He realized on the latter point, he was being selfish. If he couldn't make a real commitment to her, he needed to let her go.

He suspected she was going to walk out of his life if he didn't do something. The notion hurt and depressed him.

He paced the suite, hoping he didn't disturb people on the floor below. He tried to do some paperwork, but he couldn't stop thinking about Stella.

It was after four in the morning when he fell asleep. He woke at six when he heard his phone ring, indicating he'd received a text. Instantly awake, Aaron picked up his phone to read the message, which was from Stella.

I have very little to move. Mostly clothes. I've loaded my car and checked out. I won't need any help, but thanks anyway. I'll keep in touch and see you Tuesday evening when we go to the TCC Christmas festival.

She didn't want to see him until Tuesday evening for the party. He had a feeling that she was breaking up with him. The day after the festival would be Christmas Eve when she would fly out of Royal to go to her sister's in Austin. Aaron stared at her message. In effect, she was saying goodbye.

At least as much as she could say goodbye when she was pregnant with his baby. One thing was clear: she had moved on from spending nights with him. No more passion and lovemaking, maybe not even kisses.

He was hurt, but he could understand why she was acting this way. He should accept what she wanted. He needed to go on with his life and adjust to Stella not being a part of it.

He did some additional paperwork, then after a while picked up his phone again to make calls. Soon he had moved his Dallas appointment until later in the day so he didn't have to leave Royal as early. He showered, shaved and dressed, ordering room service for a quick breakfast while he made more calls.

He may have to tell Stella goodbye this week, but before that happened, there was one last thing he could do for her. Hurting, he picked up the phone to make another call.

As soon as the hospital allowed visitors that morning, Aaron went to see Mayor Vance.

After he finished his business in Dallas later that afternoon, Aaron went home to gather some things to take back to Royal with him. He paused to call Stella. He had tried several times during the day, but she had never answered and she didn't now.

He suspected she didn't want to talk to him, because she kept her phone available constantly in case someone in Royal needed help.

Certain he wouldn't even see her, he decided to stay at home in Dallas Friday night and go back Saturday. He wouldn't have even gone then except he had appointments in Royal all day Saturday to talk to people about the upcoming appointment of an acting mayor.

He already missed Stella and felt as if he had been away from her for a long time when it really wasn't even twenty-four hours yet.

He wondered whether she was thinking seriously about taking the Houston job offer. It would be a good job, but Aaron knew so many people in Royal wanted her to take the acting mayor position—including the mayor, who had now talked to the town council about it.

That night Aaron couldn't get her on her phone. When she didn't answer at one in the morning, he gave up, but he wondered where she was and who she was with. He missed her. She had filled an empty place in his life. He sat thinking about her—beautiful, intelligent, fun to be with, sexy— she was all that he wanted in a woman. Had he fallen in love with her without realizing it?

The idea shook him. He went to his kitchen and got a beer and then walked back to the guest bedroom downstairs where she had stayed when she had been at his house. He thought about being in bed with her, holding her in his arms.

He missed her terribly and he didn't want to tell her goodbye. It shocked him to think about it, and decided that he was in love with her. Why hadn't he seen it before now? He'd wanted to be with her day and night.

When he recognized that he loved Stella, he also saw he might be on the verge of losing her. She was a strong woman with her own standards and views and so far she had turned him down on marriage. Plus, she was considering accepting a very good position in Houston, which was a long way from Dallas.

He was in love with her and she was going to have his baby. He didn't want to lose her. He ran his hand over his short hair while he thought about what he could do to win her love. She'd accused him of proposing out of a sense of duty instead of love, which was exactly what he had done at the time. But he had spent a lot of time with her since then. There had been intimacy between them, hours together. They had worked together regarding Royal, had fun being together.

Why hadn't he seen that his feelings for her were growing stronger? He admired her; he respected and desired her. She was all the things he wanted in a woman. He had to win her love.

While he had never heard a declaration of love from Stella, she had to feel something for him. She acted as if she did. He was certain she would never have gone to bed with him with only casual feelings about him. That would be totally unlike her. Was she in love, too?

Had he already tossed away his chance with her?

He stood and moved impatiently to a window to gaze out at the lit grounds of his estate. If nothing else he would see her Tuesday night when he took her to the TCC Christmas festival. He wished he could move things up or go back to last week, but he couldn't.

He walked down the hall to his office. Crossing the room, he switched on a desk lamp and picked up a picture of his wife and child. "Paula, I've fallen in love. I think you'd approve. You'd like Stella and she would like you."

He realized that the pain of his loss had dulled slightly and he could look at Paula's picture and know that he loved Stella also. He set the picture on the desk, picked up his beer and walked out of the room, switching off the light.

He wanted to see Stella, to kiss her, to tell her he loved her. This time when he proposed, he would try to do it right. Was she going to turn him down a second time?

Next Tuesday was the TCC Christmas festival, a special time. The town was getting ready to appoint an acting mayor and they wanted Stella, but she just didn't realize how many wanted her and how sincere they were about it.

If he had lost her love, there still was something good that he could do for her.

Saturday morning Stella selected a Christmas tree, getting one slightly taller than usual. As soon as she had set it up on a table by the window across the room from her fireplace, she got out her decorations. Her phone chimed and she glanced at it to see a call from Aaron. She didn't take it. She would talk to him soon enough Tuesday night; right now she still felt on a rocky edge. Aaron could get to her too easily. She wanted to be firm when she was with him. After Tuesday night, she really didn't expect to go out with him again except in the new year when she had to talk to him about their baby.

She placed her hand on her tummy, which was still flat. Her clothes had gotten just the slightest bit tighter in the waist, but otherwise, she was having an easy pregnancy so far.

She was excited about the Christmas drive, which was going even better than she had expected. The presents were piling up at the TCC. Paige had told her that each day now, TCC members picked up presents from drop-off points around town and took them to the club to place around the big Christmas tree.

She tried to avoid thinking about Aaron, but that was impossible. She wasn't sleeping well, which wasn't good since she was pregnant. After Tuesday, maybe it would be easier to adjust because they wouldn't be in each other's lives as much.

She talked to her sister and learned their mother would be in Austin Christmas Eve, too. Stella checked again on her flight, scheduled to leave Christmas Eve and come back Christmas afternoon.

Aaron finally stopped calling on Monday and she heard nothing from him Tuesday. He must have caught on that she didn't want contact with him. She assumed he would still pick her up, but if he didn't show by six-thirty, she would go on her own. According to their earlier plans, he would come by for her at 6:15 p.m., which was early because the celebration did not begin until six-thirty. Her anticipation had dropped since she had parted with Aaron. She just wanted to get through the evening, leave the next day for Austin and try to pick up her life without Aaron.

For the first time in her life, Stella had her hair

done at the Saint Tropez Salon. The salon was on the east side of town, which had escaped most of the storm damage.

As she dressed, a glimmer of the enthusiasm she had originally experienced for the night returned. It was exciting to have a party and to know it would be so good for so many people who had been hurt in the storm. It cheered her to know that all the families would have presents and money and hope for a nice Christmas.

On a personal level, she hoped things weren't tense all evening with Aaron, but she thought both of them would have enough friends around that they could set their worries aside and enjoy the party. And Aaron might not care as much as she did that they would be saying goodbye.

She guessed Aaron would ask about her job offers. She still had not accepted the job offer in Houston. Every time she reached for the phone to talk to them, she pulled back.

Getting ready, she paused in front of the full-length mirror to look at herself. She wore the red dress she had worn before. One other new dress still hung in the closet, but the red dress was a Christmas color and it should be fine for the evening. When she put it on, the waist felt tighter. It was still comfortable, but she thought this was the last time she would wear the red dress until next winter.

Thinking it would be more appropriate for this party and also draw less attention, she wore the gold and diamond necklace. Once again, she wondered if Aaron was more interested in the person she had become after the makeover and all that had happened since, or the plain person she really was.

She made up her face as they had taught her at the salon, but when she started to put something on her lips, she stared at herself and put away the makeup, leaving her lips without any. She studied herself and was satisfied with her appearance.

She heard the buzzer and went to the door to meet Aaron. When sadness threatened to overwhelm her, she took a deep breath, thought of all the gifts people would be receiving tonight and opened the door with the certainty that this was the last time she would go out with Aaron Nichols.

Nine

Looking every inch the military man in civilian clothes, ready for a semiformal party, Aaron stood straight, handsome and neat with his short dark blond hair. Wearing a flawless navy suit and tie and a white shirt with gold cuff links, he made her heart beat faster.

"I've missed you," he said.

Her lips firmed and she tried to hang on to her emotions. "This is a night we've both looked forward to for a long time. Come in and I'll get my purse and coat."

"You're stunning, Stella," he said as he stepped inside and closed the door behind him. "I'm glad you wore your necklace."

"It's lovely, Aaron."

He studied her intently and she tilted her head, puzzled by his expression.

"So what are you thinking?"

"That you're the most gorgeous woman in the state of Texas."

His remark made her want to laugh and made her want to cry. It was a reminder of one of the reasons it was going to hurt so much to tell him goodbye. "A wee exaggeration, but thank you. I'm glad you think so."

"Tonight should be fun," he said. "Let's go enjoy the evening."

"We're early, but there may be things to do."

He pulled her close. "I don't want to mess up your makeup so I won't kiss you now, but I'm going to make up for it later."

She pulled his head down to kiss him for just a minute and then released him. "Nothing on my lips—see. I'm not messed up."

"No, you're hot, beautiful and I want you in my arms, Stella," he said in a husky voice with a solemn expression that might indicate he expected her to tell him goodbye tonight.

"C'mon, Aaron. We have a party to go to." He held her coat and then took her arm to go to his car.

When they arrived at the Texas Cattleman's Club, she was amazed to see the cars that had already filled the lot and were parked along the long drive all the way back down to the street.

"Aaron, it looks like most of the people in Royal are here. Wasn't this scheduled to start at six-thirty tonight?"

"It was. I can't believe they already have such a huge turnout."

"I never would have imagined it," she said. "I know the TCC invited everyone in Royal, but I never dreamed they would all come. Did you?"

"The town's pulled together since the storm— neighbor helping neighbor. I think everyone is interested."

"I'm surprised. This isn't what I expected."

"It's what I expected and hoped for." A valet opened the door for her and she stepped out. Aaron came around to take her arm. Once inside the clubhouse, she glanced around at the rich, dark wood, the animal heads that had been mounted long ago when it was strictly a men's club. Now women were members and there was a children's center that had a reputation for being one of the finest in Texas. They paused by a coatroom where

Aaron checked their coats and then he turned to take her arm again.

They headed for the great room that served for parties, events, dances and other club-wide activities. The sound of voices grew louder as they walked down the hall.

When they stepped inside the great room, a cheer went up, followed by thunderous applause. Stunned, Stella froze, staring at the smiling crowd. Everywhere she looked, people held signs that read, Stella for Acting Mayor, We Want Stella, and Thanks, Stella.

The TCC president, Gil Addison, appeared at her side. "Welcome, Stella."

Dazed, she tried to fathom what this was all about. She looked at Gil.

"This little surprise is to show you the support you have from the entire town of Royal. We all want you to accept the position of acting mayor until an election can be held and a new mayor chosen."

"I'm speechless," she said, smiling and waving at people.

"Stella, I have a letter from the mayor that I

want to read to you and to all," Gil said. "Let's go up to the front."

"Did you know about this?" she asked, turning to Aaron. He grinned and gave her a hug.

"A little," he said, and she realized that Aaron might have been behind organizing this gathering of townspeople.

Gil smiled. "Aaron, you come with us," Gil said, and led the way. There was an aisle cleared to the stage at the front of the room.

As she approached the stage, people greeted her and shook her hand and she smiled, thanking them. Dazed, she couldn't quell her surprise.

At the front as she climbed the three steps to the stage, more people greeted her. She shook hands with the town council and other city dignitaries. The sheriff greeted her, and the heads of different agencies in town crowded around to say hello.

"Stella, Stella, Stella," several people in the audience began chanting and in seconds, the entire room was chanting her name. She saw her friends Paige and Edie in the front row, smiling and waving.

"Mercy, Aaron, what is all this?" Dazed, embarrassed, she turned to Gil. "Gil—" She gave up trying to talk with all the chanting. Smiling, she waved at everyone.

Gil stepped forward and held up his hands for quiet. "Thanks to all of you for coming out tonight. The Texas Cattleman's Club is happy to have nearly everyone in Royal come celebrate the Christmas season and the holidays. We have a bit of business we wanted to discuss before the partying begins."

The crowd had become silent and Gil had a lapel mike so it was easy to hear him. "We have some people onstage—I imagine everyone here knows them, but in case they don't, I want to briefly tell you who is here. Please save your applause until I finish. I'll start with our sheriff, Nathan Battle." Gil ran through the list, reeling off the names of the town council members and heads of various agencies, and when he was done, the audience applauded.

"Now as you know, Mayor Vance was critically injured by the tornado. He is off the critical list—" Gil paused while people clapped. "He is still in the hospital and unable to join us tonight, but he has sent a letter for me to read, which I will do now.

'To the residents of Royal,
I am still recovering from the storm and most
deeply grateful to be alive and that my family
survived. My deepest sympathy goes out to
those who lost their loved ones, their homes,
their herds or crops. We were hurt in so many
ways, but from the first moment after the
storm, people have helped each other.
It was with deep regret that I learned that Deputy Mayor Max Rothschild was also killed
by the tornado. Since I will not be able to return to this job for a few more months, Royal
will temporarily need an acting mayor. I have
talked to our city officials, agency heads and
concerned citizens, and one name comes up
often and we are all in agreement. I hope we
can persuade Ms. Stella Daniels to accept this
position.'"

Gil paused to let people applaud and cheer. The
noise was making her ears ring. Just then, Aaron
leaned close to whisper in her ear, "I told you everyone wants you."

She smiled and threw kisses and waved, then
put her hand down, hoping Gil could calm the
crowd. She was stunned by the turnout and the

crowd's enthusiastic support—for the first time in her life, she felt accepted by everyone. She glanced at Aaron, who smiled and winked at her, and she was certain he was the one behind this crowd that had gathered.

Gil raised his hand for quiet. "Folks, there's more from Mayor Vance.

'Please persuade Ms. Stella Daniels to accept this position. Since the first moments after the storm Stella has been doing my job. Now that I have recovered enough to read the mail I receive, I have had texts, emails, letters and cards that mention Stella and all she is doing for Royal and its citizens. I urge Stella to accept this position and I am heartily supported by the town council, other officials of Royal and by its citizens.

Merry Christmas. Best wishes for your holiday,

The Honorable Richard Vance, Mayor of Royal, Texas.'"

There was another round of cheers and applause and Gil motioned for quiet. "At this point, I'm turning the meeting over to Nathan Battle."

Nathan received applause and motioned for quiet. "Thanks. I volunteered to do this part of the program. Royal needs an acting mayor." Nathan turned to Stella. "Stella, I think you can see that Mayor Vance, the town council and the whole town of Royal would like you to accept this position that will end in a few months when Mayor Vance can return to work. Will you be acting mayor of Royal?"

Feeling even more dazed, she looked up at Nathan Battle's dark brown eyes. Taking a deep breath, she smiled at him. "Yes, I'll accept the job of acting mayor until Mayor Vance gets back to work."

Her last words were drowned out by cheers and applause. Nathan shook her hand as he smiled. "Congratulations," he shouted. He stepped back and applauded as she turned and Aaron gave her a brief hug.

Everyone onstage shook her hand and tried to say a few words to her. The audience still cheered so she waved her hands for quiet.

"I want to thank all of you for this show of support. I'm stunned and amazed. I'll try my best to do what I can for Royal, as so many of you are doing. Let's all work together and, hopefully, we can get this town back in shape far sooner than anyone expected. Thank you so very much."

As the crowd applauded, Gil stepped forward and motioned for quiet again. "One more thing at this time. We can go from here to the dining hall. There's a buffet with lots of tables of food. Everyone can eat and during dessert we'll have Stella perform her first task as acting mayor and make presentations of gifts. There will be singing of Christmas carols in the dining room and then dancing back in this room, games in other rooms and the children's center will be open for the little ones. We have staff to take care of the babies. Now let's adjourn to the dining hall."

They applauded and Stella started down the steps to shake hands with people and talk to them. She lost track of Aaron until he showed up at her side and handed her a glass of ice water.

Gratefully, she sipped it and continued moving through the crowd toward the dining room. "You did this," she said to him.

"All I did was tell people we would do this tonight. No one would have come tonight if they hadn't wanted you for acting mayor and hadn't wanted to thank and support you."

"Aaron, I don't know what to say. I'm still reeling in shock."

"Congratulations. Now you'll get paid a little more for what you've been doing anyway. That's the thing, Stella. You're already doing this job and you have been for the past two months."

"If people know I'm pregnant, they might not want me for the job."

"It's most likely only for a couple more months and you're doing great so far."

"How many more surprises do you have in store tonight, Aaron?"

"I'm working on that one," he said, and she rolled her eyes. "The band is coming in now. Let's head to the dining room and nibble on something while they set up."

"I don't know how long I'm going to feel dazed."

"It'll wear off and life will go right back to normal. You'll see."

Cole suddenly appeared in front of her. "Congratulations, Stella. You deserve to have the official title since you're doing all the work that goes with it."

"Thank you for coming tonight, Cole. I appreciate everyone showing their support. I had no idea."

"Well, Aaron organized this and I'm glad to be here because you should have this position. Just keep up what you're doing," he said, smiling at her.

"Thanks so much," she said.

"I'm touched you came tonight, Cole. I'm really amazed."

"I wouldn't have missed this."

As they moved on, she leaned closer to Aaron. "I'll remember this night all my life. I'll go see Mayor Vance tomorrow and thank him. But I suppose my biggest thanks goes to you. You must have been really busy talking to everyone."

"It didn't take any persuasion on my part. Everyone thought you'd be the best person for the job."

"Well, I'm amazed and touched by that, too. I just did what needed to be done, like hundreds of other people in Royal."

Gil Addison appeared again. "Stella. As acting mayor you should take charge of the next event on tonight's schedule. We'd like to tell people to pick up their envelopes and their presents when-ever they want. Some families have little chil-dren and they won't want to stay long. Also, as acting mayor, you really should be at the head of the food line."

"I don't want to cut in front of people," she said, laughing and shaking her head. "I'll just get in line."

"Enjoy the few little perks you get with this job," Gil said. "There won't be many."

As they headed toward the dining room, peo-ple continued to stop and congratulate her. Paige walked up while the Battles talked to Aaron.

"You look gorgeous," she said. "Your necklace and bracelet are beautiful."

"Thank you. Aaron gave them to me."

"Aaron? I'm surprised, but glad Aaron is com-ing out of his shell. All our lives are changing, some in major ways, some in tiny ones, but the storm was a major upheaval for all of us. At least it looks as if we're all pulling together."

"I'm astounded, but oh, so thrilled. Thanks, Paige, for your part in this evening."

"Whatever I can do, I'm glad to. After I eat, I'll be at the table with the envelopes we're giving out. Members of the TCC will help us and we're doing this in shifts."

"Great, thanks."

Paige moved on and Aaron took Stella's arm to walk to the dining room. Enticing smells of hot bread, turkey and ham filled the air, and the dining room had three lines of long tables laden with food. The rest of the room was filled with tables covered in red or green paper where people could sit. At the back of the room was a huge decorated Christmas tree. Presents surrounded it, spilling out in front of it, lining the wall behind it. There appeared to be hundreds of wrapped presents. Paige, Lark, Edie, Megan and four TCC members sat at two tables to hand out envelopes of money some families would be receiving.

Gil appeared again. "Stella, you're the guest of honor—you get to go to the head of the line."

"I feel ridiculous doing that."

"We need you to go anyway so you can make the announcement about the gifts. Aaron, you go with her. Everyone's waiting for you to start."

Aaron took her arm as they followed Gil to the head of a line.

She had little appetite, but she ate some of the

catered food that was there in abundance—turkey, dressing, mashed potatoes and cream gravy, ham, roasts, barbecued ribs, hot biscuits, thick golden corn bread, pickled peaches, an endless variety.

When they finished, Gil excused himself and left the table. He was back in minutes to sit and lean closer to talk to Stella. "We're ready to start matching people up with their gifts. People can pick up their things all evening long until eleven-thirty. The volunteers will change shifts at regular intervals so no one has to spend the whole evening handing out presents. If you're ready, I'll announce you. Aaron, go onstage. You'll be next about the Dallas TCC."

"Sure," she said. "Excuse me," she said to Nathan Battle, who sat beside her.

At the front of the room, Gil called for everyone's attention. "As I think all of you know, some people in Royal lost everything in the storm. A good number of Royal residents have been badly hit. So many of us wanted to do something about that. This was Stella's idea and I'll let her tell you more about it—" He handed a mike to Stella.

"As you all know," Stella began, "we decided to do a Christmas drive to provide presents and support for the people who need it most. All the Texas Cattleman Club's members, along with the ladies from the Christmas-drive committee volunteered to help. Those who could do so, both from Royal and other parts of Texas have contributed generously so everyone in Royal can have a wonderful holiday.

"Each family receiving gifts tonight has been assigned a number. First, go over to the table where the volunteers are seated near the west wall and pick up the envelope that matches your number. That envelope is for you and your family. Also, there are gifts that correspond to those numbers under the Christmas tree and along the back wall. Just go see a volunteer, who will help you. You get both an envelope plus the wrapped gifts that correspond to your number.

"We want to give a huge thanks to all who contributed money, time and effort to this drive to make sure everyone has a merry Christmas. Thank you."

People applauded and Stella started to sit, but Gil appeared and motioned her to wait. He took the mike. "I have one more important announcement—some really good news for us. Aaron

Nichols and Cole Richardson are members of the Dallas, Texas, Cattleman's Club, but they are spending so much time and money in Royal trying to help us rebuild the town that the Texas Cattleman's Club of Royal invited them to join, which they did. Aaron Nichols and Cole will tell you about the rest. Aaron," Gil said, and handed the mike to Aaron while everyone applauded.

"Thanks. We're glad to help. This is Cole's hometown and I feel like it's mine now, too, because I've been here so much and everyone is so friendly. We've talked to some of our TCC friends in Dallas. I'll let Cole finish this." Aaron handed the mike to Cole, who received applause.

"It's good to be home again." He received more applause and waved his hand for quiet as he smiled. "We have friends here tonight from the Dallas TCC. They told us today that they wanted to make a presentation tonight. I want to introduce Lars West, Sam Thompkins and Rod Jenkins. C'mon, guys," he said as each man waved and smiled at the audience.

Tall with thick brown hair, Lars West stepped forward. "Thanks, Cole. We know the TCC suffered damage along with so much of Royal. We talked to our Dallas TCC and we want to present a check to the TCC here in Royal," he said, turning to Gil Addison. "We'd like the Royal TCC to have a check for two million dollars to use for Royal storm aid however the TCC here sees fit."

The last of his words were drowned out by applause as the audience came to their feet and gave him a standing ovation.

Aaron motioned to Stella to join him and he introduced her to the men from Dallas. "Thank you," she said. "That's an incredibly generous gift and will do so much good for Royal."

"We hope so. We wanted to do something," Sam said.

They talked a few more minutes and then left the stage while Cole lingered and turned to Stella.

"I was about to go home," Cole said. "I thought Aaron could do this by himself, but he talked me into staying for the presentation. There are other Dallas TCC members here for a fun night. These three guys insist on going back to Dallas tonight, so we're all leaving now," Cole told them as Gil shook hands and thanked the Dallas TCC members.

"Cole, again, thanks so much for coming out," Stella said.

"I want to thank you, too," Aaron added.

"I hope all of this tonight brightened everybody's Christmas," Cole said. He left the stage to join the TCC Dallas members, moving through the crowd. He passed near Paige Richardson, speaking to her, and she smiled, speaking in return, both of them looking cordial as they passed each other.

Gil left to put the check in a safe place. Aaron took Stella's arm to go back to the great room where a band played and people danced. People stopped to congratulate Stella, to thank her. Some thanked Aaron for the TCC Dallas contribution.

"I'm going to dance with you before we leave here," Aaron said.

"I just hope we didn't miss anyone tonight in terms of the presents and money we're giving to families."

"Everyone could sign up who felt the need and some people signed up friends who wouldn't come in and sign up themselves. I don't think anyone got overlooked, but there's no way to really know," he said. "And with that, let's close this chapter on

Royal's recovery for tonight and concentrate on you and me."

Startled, Stella looked up at him.

"Let's dance," he said, taking her into his arms. "We can't leave early, Stella. All these people came for you and they'll expect you to stay and have a good time. They'll want to speak to you."

"Aaron, in some ways," she said as she danced with him, "all my life I've felt sort of like an outsider. I've always been plain—I grew up that way and my mother is that way. For the first time tonight, I feel really accepted by everyone."

"You're accepted, believe me. Stella, people are so grateful to you. I've talked to them, and they're grateful for all you've done. And as for plain— just look in the mirror."

"You did that for me," she said solemnly, thinking the evening would have been so wonderful if she'd had Aaron's love. It was a subject she had shut out of her mind over and over since their arrival at the club tonight. Tears threatened again and she no longer felt like dancing.

"Aaron, I need a moment," she said, stepping away from him. She knew the clubhouse from being there with members for various events and she hurried off the dance floor and out of the room, heading for one of the small clubrooms that would be empty on a night like this. Tears stung her eyes and she tried to control them, wiping them off her cheeks.

A hand closed on her arm and Aaron stopped her. He saw her tears and frowned.

"C'mon," he said, holding her arm and walking down the hall to enter a darkened meeting room. Hanging a sign, Meeting in Progress, on the outside knob and switching on a small lamp, he closed the door.

She wiped her eyes frantically and took deep breaths.

He turned to face her, walking to her and placing his hands on his hips. "I was going to wait until we went home tonight to talk to you, but I think we better talk right now. What started out to be a great, fun evening for you has turned sour in a big way."

"Aaron, we can't talk here."

"Yes, we can." He stepped close and slipped one arm around her waist. His other hand tilted her chin up as he gazed into her eyes. "This is long overdue, but as the old saying goes, sometimes you can't see the forest for the trees. I've missed you and I've been miserable without you. I love you, Stella."

Startled, she frowned as she stared at him. "You're saying that—I don't think you mean it. It's one of those nice and honorable things you do."

"No. I'm not saying it to be nice and not out of honor. It's out of love. After I lost Paula and Blake, I didn't think I would ever love again. I didn't think I could. I was wrong, because there's always room in the heart for love. I just couldn't even see that I had fallen in love with you."

Shocked, she stared at him. "Aaron, I didn't know about your wife and son until this past week."

He frowned. "I thought everyone around here knew that. I just didn't talk about it."

"That's been a barrier between us, hasn't it?"

"It was, but it's not now. I'm in love with you. I want to marry you and if you'd found out today that you're not really pregnant, I would still tell you the same thing. I love you. When I lost Paula and Blake, I didn't want to live, either. I hurt every minute of every day for so long. When I finally did go out with a woman, I think it was three or four years later and after the date, I just wanted to go home and be alone."

She hurt for him, but she remained silent because Aaron was opening himself up completely to her and gone was the shuttered look and the feeling that a wall had come between them.

"I finally began to socialize, but I just never got close to anyone until you came along. I soon realized that you were the first woman I'd enjoyed being around since Paula. I also noticed I didn't hurt as much and I didn't think about her as much.

"Stella, I will always love Paula and Blake. There's room in my heart for more love—for you, for our baby. I love you and I have been miserable without you and it's my own fault for shutting you out, but I just didn't even realize I was falling in love with you."

"Aaron," she said, her happiness spilling over.

He pulled her close, leaning down to kiss her, a hungry, passionate kiss as if he had been waiting years to do this.

Joyously she clung to him and kissed him. "I love you, Aaron. I missed you, but I want your love. I just want you to be able to share the good and the bad, the hurts, the happiness, everything in your life with me and me with you. That's love, Aaron."

He held her so tightly she could barely breathe. "You mean everything to me. I just couldn't even recognize what I felt until I saw I was losing you. Thank goodness I haven't."

"No, you haven't. You have my heart. I love you, Aaron. I've loved you almost from the very first."

"Stella, wait." He knelt on one knee and held her hand. "Stella Daniels, will you marry me?" he asked, pulling a box from his jacket pocket and holding it out to her.

"Aaron." She laughed, feeling giddy and bubbly. "Yes, I'll marry you, Aaron Nichols. For goodness' sake, get up," she said, taking the box from him. "What is this, Aaron?"

She opened the box and gasped. Aaron took out the ten-carat-diamond-and-emerald ring he had bought. He held her hand and slipped the ring onto her finger. "Perfect," he said, looking into her eyes. "Everything is perfect, Stella. I will tell you I love you so many times each day you'll grow tired of hearing it."

"Impossible," she said, looking at the dazzling ring. "Oh, Aaron, I'm overwhelmed. This is the most beautiful ring. I can't believe it's mine."

"It is definitely yours. Stella, I love you. Also, I'm going to love our baby so very much. This child is a gift and a blessing for me. The loss of my first child—I can't tell you how badly that hurt and I never dreamed I'd marry and have another baby."

"We'll both be blessed by this child. I'm so glad. From the first moment, I thought this would be the biggest thrill in my life if I had your love when I found out we would have a baby."

"You have my love," he said, hugging her and then kissing her. After a few minutes, he leaned away. "C'mon. I think it's time for an announcement."

She laughed again. "Aaron, I'm used to staying in the background, being quiet and unnoticed. My life is undergoing every kind of transformation. I don't even know myself anymore in so many ways.

"I'm announcing this engagement to keep the guys away from you. I've even had them ask me if I cared if they asked you out. Yes, I cared. I wanted to punch one of them."

She laughed, shaking her head as he took her hand.

"C'mon. I'm making an announcement and then all those guys will stay away from my fiancée."

When he said *my fiancée*, joy bubbled in her as she hurried beside him.

"Stella, let's get married soon."

"You need to meet my family. I should meet yours."

"You will. I'll take you to Paris soon to meet them. Either before or after the wedding, whichever you want."

"You're changing my life in every way."

In the great room, when the band stopped between pieces, Aaron found Gil. Stella couldn't believe what was happening, but Gil motioned to the band and hurried to talk to them.

He turned to the dancers and people seated at small tables around the edge of the room. There was a roll from the drummer and people became quiet. "Ladies and gentlemen," Gil said. "May I have your attention? We have a brief announcement."

Stella shook her head. "Aaron, you started this," she said, and he grinned.

Aaron stepped forward, but Stella moved quickly to take the mike from a surprised Gil. "Folks," she said, smiling at Aaron as he took her hand. "I'd like to make my first announcement as acting mayor. I'd like to announce my engagement to Aaron Nichols," she proclaimed, laughing and looking at Aaron.

As everyone applauded and cheered, Aaron turned to slip his arm around her and kiss her briefly, causing more applause and whistles.

When he released her, he took the mike. "Now we can all go back to partying! Merry Christmas, everybody!"

There was another round of applause as the band began to play.

"Thanks, Gil," Aaron said, handing back the mike. "Let's go dance," he said to Stella. "Two dances and then we start calling family."

It was a fast piece and she danced with Aaron, having a wonderful time. She wanted him and was certain they would go home and make love. When the number ended, people crowded around them to congratulate her and look at her ring. She left the dance floor to let them and remained talking to friends until Aaron rescued her a whole number later.

"Instead of dancing some more, how about going to your place?"

"I'll beat you to the door," she said, teasing him, and he laughed. "I have to get my purse and start thanking people."

"Everybody is partying. Save the thank-you for one you can write on a Christmas card or wedding announcement or something."

"You're right about everyone partying," she said. "You win. Let's go."

He took her hand and she got her purse. They stopped to get their coats and then at the door they waited while a valet brought Aaron's car.

Everybody who passed them congratulated her on becoming acting mayor and on her engagement.

When they drove away from the club, she turned toward him slightly. It was quiet and cozy in his car. "Aaron, this has been the most wonderful night of my life," she said. "Thanks to you."

"I'm glad. Let's have this wedding soon."

"That's what I'd like."

"I don't care whether we have a large or small one."

"My parents will want no part of a large wedding. I got my plain way of life from my mother."

"If you prefer a large wedding, have it. I'll pay for it and help you."

She squeezed his knee lightly. "Thank you. That's very nice. What about you?"

"I don't care. Mom and Dad will do whatever we want. So will my brother."

"Probably a small wedding and maybe a large reception. After tonight, I feel I have to invite the entire town of Royal to the reception."

"I agree. That was nice of everyone. All the people I talked to were enthused, everybody wanted you to be acting mayor. Stella, I didn't find anyone who didn't want you. Mayor Vance definitely wanted you."

"That makes me feel so good. I can't tell you. In high school I was sort of left out of things socially. I guess I always have been."

"Not now. You'll never be left out of anything with me."

"I think you're speeding. I'd hate for the new

acting mayor to get pulled over the first few hours I have the job."

"I want to get home to be alone with you," he said as he slowed.

In minutes they reached her town house. "My trunk is filled with Christmas gifts. I'm not carrying them in tonight. I'll get them in the morning," he said.

"I have to go shopping tomorrow. I've been so busy I haven't gotten all my presents and I don't have any for you yet. I really didn't expect to be with you Christmas."

"But now you will be if I can talk you into it. How disappointed will your sister be if you don't come this year and we spend Christmas here, just the two of us?"

"With three kids, she won't care. We can go sometime during the holidays. We can call her."

"We sure can, but later. I have other plans when I close the door."

"Do you really?" she teased.

He parked where she directed him to and came around to open her door. As soon as they stepped into her entryway, Aaron closed the door behind him and turned to pull her into his embrace, giving a kiss that was filled with love and longing.

Later Stella lay in his arms while he toyed with her hair. The covers were pulled up under her arms.

Aaron stretched out his arm to pick up his phone and get a calendar. "Let's set a date now."

"Aaron," she said, trailing her fingers along his jaw, "since I just accepted the job of acting mayor, I feel a responsibility for Royal. I'll have to live here until I'm no longer acting mayor."

"I'm here all the time anyway. I'll work from here and go to Dallas when I feel I need to. We can build a house here if you want. Remember, that is my business."

"Whatever you'd like. When my job ends, I don't mind moving to Dallas."

"We'll work it all out. I just want to be with you."

"Our honeymoon may have to come after baby is here," she said.

"Baby is here," he echoed. "Stella, I've told you before and I'll tell you again—I'm overjoyed about the baby. I lost Blake and he was one of the big loves of my life. I have a second chance here to be a dad. I'm thrilled and I hope you are."

"I am. Do you particularly want another little boy?"

"No, I don't care," he said, and she smiled, relieved and happy that he didn't have his heart set on having a boy.

"Just a baby. I can't tell you." His voice had gotten deep and she realized he was emotional about the baby he'd lost. She hugged him and rose up to kiss him, tasting a salty tear. His hurt caused her heart to ache. "Aaron, I'm so glad about this baby. And we can have more."

He pulled her down to kiss her hard. When he released her, she saw he had a better grip on his emotions. "For a tough, military-type guy, you're very tenderhearted," she said.

"I am thrilled beyond words to be a dad. That's why I got those necklaces for you. I love you, Stella."

"I love you," she responded.

"Now let's set a date for a wedding. How about a wedding between Christmas and New Year's? That's a quiet time. January won't be."

"You're right. I'd say a very quiet wedding after Christmas. Can you do that, Mr. Nichols?"

"I can. Want to fly to Dallas next week to get a wedding dress from Cecilia? That'll be a Christmas present to you."

She smiled. "Your love is my Christmas present. Your love, your baby, this fabulous ring. Aaron, I love you with all my heart. I give you my love for Christmas." Joy filled her while she looked into his brown eyes.

"Merry, merry Christmas, darling," he said as he wrapped his arms around her and pulled her close to kiss her.

Happiness filled her heart and after a moment she looked up at him. "Your love is the best Christmas gift possible." She felt joyous to be in Aaron's strong arms and to know she had his love always.

* * * * *

MILLS & BOON®

Why shop at millsandboon.co.uk?

Each year, thousands of romance readers find their perfect read at millsandboon.co.uk. That's because we're passionate about bringing you the very best romantic fiction. Here are some of the advantages of shopping at www.millsandboon.co.uk:

* **Get new books first**—you'll be able to buy your favourite books one month before they hit the shops

* **Get exclusive discounts**—you'll also be able to buy our specially created monthly collections, with up to 50% off the RRP

* **Find your favourite authors**—latest news, interviews and new releases for all your favourite authors and series on our website, plus ideas for what to try next

* **Join in**—once you've bought your favourite books, don't forget to register with us to rate, review and join in the discussions

Visit **www.millsandboon.co.uk**
for all this and more today!